The Adventures of Kitty Wappis

Written by Jon Sniderman
Illustrated by Javier Duarte

ISBN 978-1-936046-66-9
1-936046-66-0

Published by Mirror Publishing
Milwaukee, WI 53214
www.pagesofwonder.com

Printed in the USA.

This is a work of fiction. Names, titles, characters, events, locations, and incidents are the product of the author's imagination. Any resemblance to actual persons, places, locations, animals, or other things, either living or dead, is purely coincidental. No animals were harmed during the creation of this book.

The name, KITTY WAPPIS, originated when my grandfather, Grandpa (name omitted to protect the innocent) slurred the words KITTY WAMPUS because he was always chewing on a cigar. Anything appearing to him to be crooked, out of alignment, or tilted (which may have been quite often) solicited a slurred version of KITTY WAMPUS. Every time I had heard this (I may have been 5 or 6 years old at the time) it sounded like KITTY WAPPIS. You have my grandfather to thank for this creation.

Many thanks to my family and friends for their undying support. Their suggestions were certainly unparalled! Many of the names, locales, and events were derived from their imaginations. Some of their names are actually used in the stories. They know who they are! Much love to them all!

G'pa Jon

The author lives with his wife, Fran, and their attack cat, Tabitha. The author retired from the University of Michigan and currently resides in southeast Michigan

Dedicated to my children and their children

KIMBERLY & ALEX	JEFF & SHELBY	TRACY & JASON
JAKE	ETHAN	JORDAN
SAMANTHA	MADISON	MORGAN
JACOB	BRENNA	GABRIEL
MEGAN	LILY	

Table of Contents

Episode One: THE BEGINNING

It all began a very long time ago in the little village of Sticky Wicket. In case you don't know where Sticky Wicket is, just venture to beautiful downtown Bumpershoots. At the blinking red light in the very center of downtown STOP very quickly! (You really can't miss the red blinking light because it is the only red blinking light in the whole town of Bumpershoots!) Very quietly LOOK to the right! Then, LOOK to the left! LOOK up! LOOK down. LOOK behind you! LOOK under you! LOOK all around! When you are sure that no one is watching, turn yourself catty corner and follow the stone path. Soon, if you do not get distracted by the beautiful flowers and trees, you will get to Sticky Wicket.

Sticky Wicket is only a stone's throw....well, perhaps just a couple minutes of pacing, skipping, or dancing, from Kitty Village. If you had not turned catty corner in beautiful downtown Bumpershoots, then you probably would have gone to Kitty Village! The two villages are very close to each other to be sure! Just remember to always turn catty corner and follow the stone path to get to Sticky Wicket!

Kitty Wappis was born in Sticky Wicket. He had many brothers and sisters. Perhaps you may have heard of the Feline movie star and model, Miss Jor-Dan Wappis? Very famous, indeed! Oh yes, we cannot forget the other famous sister, Miss Mor-Gan Wappis. She is a famous Feline Ballet star, part time acrobat, and mountain climber! She is always traveling and climbing this mountain, then that mountain, or dancing in this part of the world, then dancing in a different part of the world! Are you sure you haven't heard of them somewhere?

When Kitty Wappis was very young he would play with his brothers and sisters. They would run up and down the big tree in the yard. They would tangle themselves in yarn! They would play tag and, just generally, had fun like you do!

Soon, as time slipped by (it only seemed like yesterday!), it was time to go to pre-school. Kitty Wappis and his brothers and sisters were all born at the same time so they were all the same age. Because they were all the same age, they all got to go to pre-school together. Wasn't that nice?

Pre-school was only two blocks away. Their mother would make a parade of all the children. Sometimes she would pick one of her kittens to lead the parade! What fun it was!

This was a very special pre-school just for kittens! Its name was: "The Sticky Wicket Purr-fect KittyGarden School".

There were lots of kittens at the pre-school! There were lots of toys and books! There were lots of things to learn and do, too! It was a very nice pre-school!

Kitty Wappis made lots of friends at his new school! He met Andrew, and Billy, and Charley, and Titus, and Danielle, and Loretta, and many, many, more new friends.

Kitty Wappis was a very smart kitten! He learned the alphabet and his numbers very quickly! He learned to read, too! Kitty Wappis could put jigsaw puzzles together lickety split!

Kitty Wappis learned that all the special books, like mathematics and the sciences, were on the top shelves. Kitty Wappis taught himself to stretch up on the very tips of his hind feet then swish his tail for balance to reach these books! Then, he would use his front paws to remove the books from the shelves. Kitty Wappis taught himself to hold the books while standing upright on his hind feet. Sometimes, he would even use his little whiskers to turn the pages! Kitty Wappis was a very talented kitty cat, wasn't he?

Kitty Wappis, also, was a very strange kitty cat. Kitty Wappis taught himself how to walk upright on his hind feet with his tail swishing back and forth and from side to side. Sometimes, when he walked upright, his upper torso would lean. Sometimes, he would LEAN to the right. Sometimes, he would LEAN to the left.

Sometimes, when his tail was on the same side he was leaning, one would think that he would just fall over….but, he never did!

Kitty Wappis was soon graduated from school. He had advanced very quickly because he was so smart! Now it was time to leave home and school and begin new adventures!

THIS WAS A SPECIAL DAY FOR STICKY WICKET!

Many people came to Sticky Wicket to adopt the various animals. People came by bicycles and motorcycles. People came by automobiles and trains! One daring fellow even came by parachute! (How did he get home again?)

On this particular warm, sunny day, Kitty Wappis was walking upright and reading the newspaper. As he was crossing the street he wasn't paying any attention to the cars!

HONK!! HONK!!! SQUEAL!! SQUEAL!!

The horn blared! The tires skidded the car to a stop!! The big, black automobile stopped right in the middle of the street!

Kitty Wappis FLEW into the air! His body was leaning side to side so fast, he looked like a butterfly flapping its wings! His tail was STRAIGHT out! His back was ARCHED! The newspaper flew apart! All the hair on his back STOOD UP! His whiskers SLICED the air like lightning flashes! KITTY WAPPIS FLEW SO FAR INTO THE SKY THAT HE DID THREE SOMERSAULTS AND A PERFECT SWAN DIVE ON THE WAY DOWN!

Kitty Wappis landed on the front seat of that big, black automobile! (It certainly was a good thing the car didn't have a roof!). Kitty Wappis landed on all four of his feet (everyone knows that kitty cats always land on their feet!)

Kitty Wappis was still trying to catch his breath and calm his frazzled nerves when a hand touched his head. Kitty Wappis looked up (after his eyes could properly focus) and saw a very strange looking man. The man was quite pudgy. He wore red sunglasses! He had lots of red hair! He had a white beard! He was wearing a plaid suit with a very bright yellow vest!

Kitty Wappis looked at the strange man! The strange man looked at the strange kitty cat! Kitty Wappis wasn't sure what to do! The strange man wasn't sure what to do, either! The strange man put his hand on Kitty Wappis and patted his head. They seemed to like each other instantly…isn't that strange?

Kitty Wappis learned that this strange man in the big, black automobile was Mr. Alexander P. Frockmorton III (The third!). He was delighted to adopt Kitty Wappis!

Mr. Alexander P. Frockmorton III lived in the city in a tall house. Kitty Wappis liked this house! It had a library with lots of books and a fireplace! Kitty Wappis even had a room for himself with his own special cushion! The window in his room had a large sill with soft pillows. Kitty Wappis could sit in the sunlight in the morning and read….and nap….and read…and nap. Catnaps, maybe?

Mr. Alexander P. Frockmorton III had a very nice neighbor. He liked kitty cats, too! His name was Mr. J. Cobb (G.O.E.). (He always used the G.O.E. after his name to tell people that he was retired from working full time. The letters meant "Gentleman Of Ease") Mr. J. Cobb (G.O.E.) was a retired master wood craftsman. He had built the library for Mr. Alexander P. Frockmorton III.

Mr. J. Cobb (G.O.E.) would care for Kitty Wappis when Mr. Alexander P. Frockmorton III was traveling for his job. Mr. J. Cobb (G.O.E.) and Kitty Wappis could read books together and do some science projects, too!

Kitty Wappis was a very fortunate kitty cat. He had two new friends and a room with a cozy windowsill. He had a library full of books. He had a very nice life - until one day when he was on a cushion in the windowsill when the sun went behind a BIG, DARK CLOUD...

Not quite the end of a purr-fect adventure.......

Episode Two: KITTY SAVES A FRIEND

Kitty Wappis was on the very edge of his soft cushion on the windowsill one day when a series of events occurred. First, the sun went behind a very dark cloud. Next, it became very windy.

Then, some very, very, big raindrops began to pound against the window! All of a sudden there was a tremendous flash of lightning so close to Kitty Wappis that it actually curled the hair on his back as it hit the transformer on the pole just outside his window! As soon as that transformer exploded.......

A BONE JARRING, HEART STOPPING, *KKAABBOOOOMMM* of thunder rolled and rattled through the air!! It shook Kitty Wappis right off his cushion and threw him straight through the hallway and into the den. It plopped him down right smack on top of some letters in the middle of the desk belonging to Mr. J. Cobb (G.O.E.)!

Although the lights went out because of the lightning strike, the fireplace logs were glowing...and...well, everyone knows that kitty cats can see in the dark anyway. Kitty Wappis saw a familiar name on the letter he had landed on so abruptly. It was from an old friend from a neighborhood just on the other side of town.

Kitty Wappis and this friend had attended pre-school together. They were the best of friends until Kitty Wappis came to live with Mr. Alexander P. Frockmorton III in his very tall house and Mr. J. Cobb (G.O.E.) in the house next door.

Kitty Wappis was a very smart kitty cat. He had learned the alphabet and his numbers very quickly. He taught himself to read. He could do the crossword puzzle in the morning newspaper. He could do jigsaw puzzles lickety split!

Kitty Wappis read the letter he had landed on…right smack in the middle of the desk! Kitty Wappis then became very sad. His friend must leave the household where she has been living. She had lived there almost as long as Kitty Wappis had lived with his new friends. Kitty's friend had no other home to go to.

Kitty Wappis stopped crying. Kitty Wappis looked around the room (don't forget, kitty cats can see in the dark). Kitty Wappis has two houses. Kitty Wappis has a special room with a big window with big soft cushions. Kitty Wappis has two very special friends – Mr. Alexander P. Frockmorton III and Mr. J. Cobb (G.O.E.).

Kitty Wappis had an idea! Kitty Wappis will save his friend! Kitty Wappis would be delighted to share everything he has to save his friend (wouldn't you?).

Kitty Wappis was a very strange kitty cat. Kitty Wappis could walk upright on his hind feet with his tail swishing back and forth and from side to side. Sometimes, when he walked upright, his upper torso would lean. Sometimes, he would LEAN to the right. Sometimes, he would LEAN to the left. Sometimes, when his tail was on the same side he was leaning, one would think that he would just fall over….. but, he never did!

Tonight, in the dark, Kitty Wappis carried a small suitcase – he didn't know how long he might be gone. He brought his pajamas, a change of clothes, and his toothbrush. He also carried a little umbrella! Kitty Wappis was a very peculiar kitty cat, indeed! Tonight was very special, and tonight he would save his friend!

It started to rain a bit harder so Kitty Wappis opened his umbrella. Imagine, if you can, a kitty cat walking upright on his hind legs, leaning to the right, then leaning to the left, with his tail swishing back and forth and from side to side, and carrying an umbrella and a suitcase!

Kitty Wappis was quite a sight to see!

Kitty Wappis remembered the neighborhood and soon located the correct house. (Kitty Wappis had written down the address from the envelope on the desk.)

Kitty Wappis ducked under the awning of the front window and looked inside. There was his friend! She was curled in a ball in front of the fireplace fast asleep! She was just as Kitty Wappis remembered her! What a lucky day, indeed!

Kitty Wappis tapped on the windowpane with his umbrella. His friend put her nose up and opened one eye. Kitty Wappis tapped on the windowpane again. Then her other eye opened. Her ears stood straight up! All of a sudden she jumped to her feet and leaped to the windowsill!

She was very excited to see her friend!

Kitty Wappis purred like never before because he was so happy! Kitty's friend purred very loudly, too! Soon they were talking and Kitty's friend said that was she very thankful to have such a nice friend! She collected her clothes and toothbrush and met Kitty Wappis outside.

Kitty Wappis had saved his friend and they were as happy as could be!

As they left the house both kitty cats were smiling. Have you ever seen TWO kitty cats smile?

The end of another purr-fect adventure.

Episode Three: THE NEW BIRTHDATE PARTY

Kitty Wappis was a very lucky kitty cat! His two friends where he lived thought that Kitty Wappis should have a connecting bridge between the two houses. Mr. Alexander P. Frockmorton III lived in the taller house. Mr. J. Cobb (G.O.E.) lived in the house next door. Mr. J. Cobb (G.O.E.) was a retired master wood craftsman. He could build the new bridge for Kitty Wappis.

Kitty Wappis was a very strange kitty cat so the special bridge had to be extra wide and extra tall! Kitty Wappis could walk upright on his hind feet with his tail swishing back and forth and from side to side. Sometimes, when he walked upright, his upper torso would lean. Sometimes, he would LEAN to the right. Sometimes, he would LEAN to the left. Sometimes, when his tail was on the same side he was leaning, one would think that he would just fall over…but, he never did!

The new bridge was just the right size!

Kitty Wappis was also a very smart kitty cat! Kitty Wappis read books and did some science projects with Mr. Alexander P. Frockmorton III. Kitty Wappis could do crossword puzzles, too!

Sometimes, he did jigsaw puzzles lickety split!

On this particular day, Kitty Wappis had just finished his mid-morning catnap in his newly built bridge with lots of windows and a nicely warmed cushion. He awoke just in time to hear the postman deliver the mail. Kitty Wappis always sorted the mail. He usually read the journals and magazines!

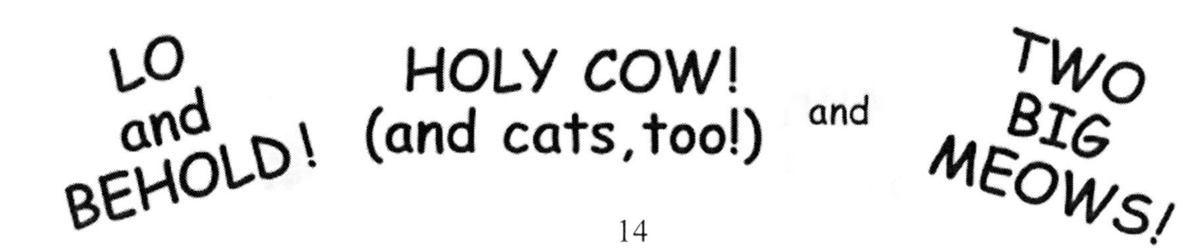

There was an envelope addressed to Kitty Wappis!

SIRE K. WAPPIS
c/o Mr. J. Cobb
City Park

WHAT A PLEASANT SURPRISE!

Kitty Wappis studied the envelope. The return address showed that it wasn't from too far away! Being curious as a kitty cat (which, of course, he was), Kitty Wappis opened the envelope. It was an invitation to a birthday party!

The invitation was from the friend he had saved and brought home with him. Her owners were leaving the city and she could not go with them. Kitty Wappis had found her a nice home. The home had two very nice children to look after her. The children (Samantha and Jake) re-named her KoKo. It had been a whole year since KoKo came to live with them. They thought it would be a good idea to celebrate with a "New Birthdate Party"!

They invited Sherlock.
They invited Spurlock.
They invited Titus.
They invited Kitty Wappis.

What a marvelous surprise for Kitty Wappis!

The "New Birthdate Party" was one week away. Kitty Wappis must get a haircut! Kitty Wappis must get his nails trimmed! Kitty Wappis definitely needed to have his whiskers groomed, too! Kitty Wappis called his veterinarian for a RUSH appointment! Luckily, there had been a cancellation and Dr. Paul could see him the next day!

Kitty Wappis was so delighted that he did a little dance! Have you ever seen a kitty cat dance?

The day of the "New Birthdate Party" soon arrived. Kitty Wappis was very excited! He couldn't wait to get there! It wasn't very far away and Kitty Wappis knew all the short cuts! He could almost see the house from his special bridge!

Kitty Wappis tucked the present (a play toy with just a hint of catnip in it) under his arm and began his journey.

Kitty Wappis was a very strange kitty cat. Kitty Wappis could walk upright on his hind feet with his tail swishing back and forth and from side to side. His present was tucked carefully under his arm. Sometimes, when he walked upright, his upper torso would lean. Sometimes, he would LEAN to the right. Sometimes, he would LEAN to the left. Sometimes, when his tail was on the same side he was leaning, one would think that he would just fall over…but, he never did!

Kitty Wappis arrived at his friend's house right on time. It was nice to see his friends again! They played lots of games! KoKo enjoyed her presents and had a delicious "New Birthdate Party" cake. It had one large candle in the very middle! Kitty Wappis even got to have his favorite ice cream for dessert. His favorite was PURPLE ice cream! What is your favorite ice cream flavor?

After dessert, the kitty cats told many stories. One might call these stories "Cat tales"! Some were very funny! What is your favorite "cat tale"?

Soon the party was over. The kitty cats helped clean up. Then, it was time to say good byes. Kitty Wappis thanked Samantha and Jake for inviting him to the "New Birthdate Party" for his friend.

Kitty Wappis was very happy for his friends! He was especially happy for KoKo! He was so happy that he smiled all the way home! Have you ever seen a kitty cat smile?

The end of another purr-fect adventure.

Episode Four: THE UNIQUE INVITATION

Kitty Wappis was very tired from all his exercising. Although he was practicing to earn the Yellow Scarf in Feline Karate, he liked to stay in tiptop mental and physical condition. You, too? After earning the Yellow scarf, Kitty Wappis could begin preparing himself for the next step- the coveted Black Scarf, 3rd degree – the very highest level in Feline Karate. It would take a lot of hard work and a very rigorous training schedule! But, right now would be a great time for his mid-morning catnap. The sun was shining and it should have had enough time by now to warm his cushion – in his special bridge with lots of windows!

Kitty Wappis climbed to his special bridge and stretched out his little toe to test the temperature of his cushion. HMmm, JUST RIGHT! Kitty Wappis tiptoed onto his cushion, turned around twice, and plopped down right smack in the middle of the sunbeam! He curled into a ball, tucked his nose under his tail, closed his eyes, and went instantly asleep. Can you fall asleep that fast?

This afternoon a new computer was to be delivered and installed in the den of the house belonging to Mr. Alexander P. Frockmorton III. He was a very best friend to Kitty Wappis. Mr. Alexander P. Frockmorton III had adopted Kitty Wappis from Sticky Wicket, the village where Kitty Wappis was born and raised.

Kitty Wappis was a very smart kitty cat. Mr. Alexander P. Frockmorton III and Kitty Wappis did many things together. They did science projects and crossword puzzles and jigsaw puzzles and read many books! They often shared the morning newspaper....but Kitty Wappis usually did the crossword puzzle by himself!

Just as the large, old Grandfather clock in the main hallway struck twelve, the door bell rang. The computer installers were here! Kitty Wappis couldn't wait! Their computer was very old!

Kitty Wappis watched as the old computer was removed and the new one installed. The installers explained everything to Mr. Alexander P. Frockmorton III. (They certainly wouldn't explain it to a kitty cat!). The CPU went there. The monitor went here! The printer should go over there! The speakers and the keyboard and the mouse go here. Soon it was all in place and connected. The new system was turned on and fully tested. The installers left and Mr. Alexander P. Frockmorton III and Kitty Wappis first checked for any messages........

There was a message from Samantha and Jake! How exciting! Samantha and Jake were the new owners of the friend Kitty Wappis had taken in when the other owners had to relocate and the kitty cat wasn't allowed to go with them. KoKo was delighted to live with Samantha and Jake!

Samantha, Jake, and KoKo were inviting Kitty Wappis and Mr. Alexander P. Frockmorton III on a field trip to the Planetarium and Observatory. The Observatory was viewing the full moon. It was to be a special night for people and their pets!

Kitty Wappis and Mr. Alexander P. Frockmorton III had accepted the invitation and were on their way to meet Samantha, Jake, and KoKo. It was a beautiful, warm, star-filled evening and the full moon was very bright. Kitty Wappis was very anxious to see the full moon through the large telescope.

Kitty Wappis and Mr. Alexander P. Frockmorton III were quite a sight to see! Mr. Alexander P. Frockmorton III was wearing his bright red tie and a yellow vest under his plaid sport jacket. He carried a walking stick that clicked on the sidewalk every time he took a step. Kitty Wappis was walking upright on his hind feet with his tail swishing back and forth and from side to side. Sometimes, when he walked upright, his upper torso would lean. Sometimes, he would LEAN to the right. Sometimes, he would LEAN to the left. Sometimes, when his tail was on the same side he was leaning, one would think that he would just fall over.... but, he never did!

Somehow, the two of them achieved the correct rhythm. Click! went the walking stick on the sidewalk and Kitty Wappis would LEAN to the right. Click! went the walking stick on the sidewalk and Kitty Wappis would LEAN to the left! Click! LEAN! Click! LEAN! Click! LEAN! TAP! and a tail swish to the right! TAP! and a tail swish to the left! Quite a sight to see, indeed!

A few people and their pets at a time were led into the room with the massive telescope. A motor was activated and the domed roof opened. The Director explained that whatever area of the moon the telescope was pointing to would be projected onto a huge screen on the wall. Kitty Wappis, Mr. Alexander P. Frockmorton III, Samantha, Jake, and KoKo were truly amazed! They had never seen the face of the moon this close before! They could see the hills and valleys and craters! They could even see the area where the astronauts had landed!

They all stopped at the souvenir shop on the way out and actually touched some moon rocks brought back by the astronauts! They all had a wonderful visit to the Observatory and Planetarium!

Kitty Wappis thanked Samantha, Jake, and KoKo for inviting him. Kitty Wappis would certainly remember this visit every time he watched the full moon set in the very early mornings!

Kitty Wappis actually smiled all the way home. Have you ever seen a kitty cat smile?

The end of another purr-fect adventure.

Episode Five: THE REUNION

Kitty Wappis, Mr. Alexander P. Frockmorton III, and Mr. J. Cobb (G.O.E.) sat down to dinner one evening. It was a Birthday dinner for Mr. Alexander P. Frockmorton III. Kitty Wappis and Mr. J. Cobb (G.O.E.) were the invited guests!

Kitty Wappis could have his favorite foods. He was especially fond of wild rice, kumquat pudding, and purple ice cream.

Mr. J. Cobb (G.O.E.)[The G.O.E. meant that Mr. J. Cobb was retired from working full time. The letters meant "Gentleman Of Ease"] could have his favorite foods, too. He especially liked hickory smoked ham with a tart cherry glazing. He loved Granny Smith apples stuffed with brown sugar and raisins and baked in the oven. Scrumptious! His favorite dessert was red chocolate cake drizzled with chocolate syrup and chocolate ice cream with a cherry on top! Yummy! Sometimes, he like whipped cream on top of his ice cream, too! Is that your favorite, too?

Mr. Alexander P. Frockmorton III had his favorite foods, too. He liked Bar-B-Que ribs, mashed potatoes, salad, and baby carmelized onions. For dessert, he liked butter pecan ice cream with some chocolate syrup and peanuts on top! (Well, maybe a spoonful of whipped cream, too!)

Kitty Wappis, Mr. Alexander P. Frockmorton III, and Mr. J. Cobb (G.O.E.) had a wonderful time. They talked and laughed and completely forgot about the time. As soon as the big, old Grandfather clock in the hallway struck seven times, they realized that they must hurry.

Mr. Alexander P. Frockmorton III certainly did not want to be late for his cooking class! Mr. J. Cobb (G.O.E.) certainly didn't want to be late for his class either. HE WAS THE TEACHER! Kitty Wappis certainly didn't want to be late for his class, either. Being late was inexcusable! Being late tonight would mean that he would not be able to participate in his Feline Karate class. He was to test this evening for the Yellow Scarf – a great feat, indeed, for a kitty cat! Kitty Wappis had trained and practiced very hard. (Can you imagine a kitty cat training for a Karate class?)

Kitty Wappis was a very strange kitty cat. Kitty Wappis could walk upright on his hind feet with his tail swishing back and forth and from side to side. Sometimes, when he walked upright, his upper torso would lean. Sometimes, he would LEAN to the right. Sometimes, he would LEAN to the left. Sometimes, when his tail was on the same side he was leaning, one would think that he would just fall over.... but, he never did!

Kitty Wappis set out for his Karate class. It was being taught at the Y.K.A. building. (YKA means "Young Kitten Association"). The YKA building was only a few blocks east and two blocks south...just, sort-of, well...maybe 'round the corner from...not but a stone's throw...anyways, not very far from the special bridge and the house belonging to Mr. J. Cobb (G.O.E.)!

Kitty Wappis had put on his Feline Karate uniform and started out as usual. He looked very strange strutting down the street. His tail was swishing back and forth and from side to side. Sometimes, he was REALLY leaning to the right and practicing some Feline Karate moves. Sometimes, he REALLY leaned to the left and practiced other Feline Karate moves. Sometimes, when his tail was on the same side he was REALLY leaning...and practicing Feline Karate moves.....well, you know what almost happens, don't you?

Kitty Wappis was very anxious to get to his class. He was so excited that he was not paying any attention to where he was going. Kitty Wappis stepped off the sidewalk.........

HONK!!! HONK!!! The horn **BLARED!! SQUEAL!! SCREACH!!**
S - Q - U - E - A - L!!!!
THE TIRES SQUEALED VERY LOUDLY!!

The big automobile veered away! Kitty Wappis almost got hit by that car! Luckily, he jumped back just in time! WHEW! Another split second and Kitty

Wappis would have been a hood ornament! Needless to say, Kitty Wappis went the rest of the way to class very carefully!

Kitty Wappis passed his test! Kitty Wappis wore his new Yellow Scarf very proudly!

Kitty Wappis stayed a bit longer to watch some of the beginner classes.

All of a sudden his ears perked WWWWAAAYYY up! His tail stopped swishing! His whiskers stood straight out! He studied two of the beginners in the class. They looked very familiar but he just couldn't remember.......until they turned around! They were his sisters!! Both of them!! It was Miss Jor-Dan and Miss Mor-Gan! WHAT A PLEASANT SURPRISE! What a marvelous reunion! They hugged and hugged each other! It had been a long time since they had seen one another! They talked and talked. Then, they even talked some more!

Soon it was time too say their good-byes. Kitty Wappis said his good-byes and left for his home. He wore his newly earned Yellow Scarf and his Feline Karate uniform very proudly.

Tonight, Kitty Wappis was smiling from ear to ear. Have you ever seen a kitty cat smile?

The end of another purr-fect adventure.

Episode Six: THE INVESTIGATIVE CONSULTANT

Kitty Wappis finished his breakfast a little early this morning. The crossword puzzle in the morning paper was very easy this time. He usually does the puzzle last. Then, the sun has a chance to warm his cushion – in his special bridge with lots of windows. Perhaps he should practice some of his Feline Karate moves and maneuvers. Soon he will begin the special training necessary to earn the coveted Black Scarf, 3rd degree – the very highest level! Kitty Wappis had worked very hard to earn his Yellow Scarf earlier this year.

Kitty Wappis started to practice playing his three-ba! musical instrument. Have you ever heard of a three-ba! musical instrument?....A One-ba?....A Four-ba?....a Two-ba(Tuba)? The three-ba! musical instrument IS very rare. Kitty Wappis taught himself to play it! Kitty Wappis was a very smart kitty cat!

After a while, the sun had time to warm his cushion – in the special bridge with lots of windows. Kitty Wappis carefully placed his three-ba! musical instrument into its case and climbed to his cushion.

Kitty Wappis stretched out his little toe to test the temperature of his cushion. HMMmmm, JUST PERFECT! He tiptoed onto his cushion, turned around twice, and plopped down right smack in the middle of the sunbeam. He curled into a ball, tucked his nose under his tail, closed his eyes, and went instantly asleep. Can you fall asleep that fast?

Kitty Wappis was an excellent dreamer. You, too?

Kitty Wappis could see an ocean and some swaying palm trees on an island. He also saw a long skinny length of sandy beach. Kitty Wappis seemed to be in some sort of hotel room with Mr. J. Cobb (G.O.E.), one of his best friends. He seemed to be high in the sky and looking down at everything. Mr. J. Cobb (G.O.E.)

was ordering some food to be delivered to room #1306 – the thirteenth floor! THE THIRTEENTH FLOOR!!! (Many hotels didn't even have a floor number 13 – it was a superstitious number meaning that many people had fears about the number 13…especially in a hotel!).

Kitty Wappis wandered around the room. He found a notebook with what appeared to be his hand (paw?) writing in it. (Remember, Kitty Wappis was a very good dreamer!) The written words told of a mysterious disappearance of some green slippers belonging to the sister of Mr. J. Cobb.

The sister was telling the hotel security people that the slippers were very valuable. She had last seen them in the closet but they were either lost or stolen now!

Kitty Wappis checked everywhere in the room. He used his powerful magnifying glass and studied the carpet. He found some very strange small pieces of something that looked like….like feathers! The slippers could not have walked out by themselves….or could they? (It was still a dream, you know!) A mystery for sure! Right?

Kitty Wappis was looking out the window while in deep thought about the missing slippers, and stroking his whiskers for ideas. Then, he developed a theory! He put away his magnifying glass and pulled out his collapsible telescope from his KITTY WAPPIS INVESTIGATIVE CONSULTANT suitcase. He opened his telescope one click at a time while looking at those swaying palm trees on the island. Another click, and the island got closer. Click! Click! Click!...and each time the island and the trees became closer and closer. Click! Click! Click! went the telescope and the birds became larger and larger! The birds were fighting over some fuzzy green things!

LO and BEHOLD! HOLY COW! (and cats, too!) and TWO BIG MEOWS!

Kitty Wappis had found the missing slippers! The birds in the swaying tree tops must have flown into the room (on the thirteenth floor!) and swooped up the very valuable slippers belonging to the sister of Mr. J. Cobb (G.O.E.)

Kitty Wappis handed his telescope to the hotel security people and pointed toward the swaying tree tops on the island in the ocean. The security people were amazed! Mr. J. Cobb (G.O.E.) and his sister were amazed, too! Kitty Wappis had solved the case of the missing slippers!

The security people had never seen a kitty cat like Kitty Wappis! Kitty Wappis was a very strange kitty cat. Kitty Wappis could walk upright on his hind feet with his tail swishing back and forth and from side to side. Sometimes, when he walked upright, his upper torso would lean. Sometimes, he would LEAN to the right. Sometimes, he would LEAN to the left. Sometimes, when his tail was on the same side he was leaning, one would think that he would just fall over.... but, he never did!

Kitty Wappis was so happy that he smiled all the way down the hallway! Have you ever seen a kitty cat smile?

Then, he awoke from his dream.

The end of another purr-fect adventure.

Draw a picture of the green slippers and the birds in the swaying trees.

Episode Seven: THE BUILDING PROJECT

Kitty Wappis had just finished the crossword puzzle in the morning newspaper. It was usually the last thing he did before it was time for his mid-morning catnap. He had watched the full moon set in the western sky very early this morning. He did some jigsaw puzzles, too. He could do those lickety split! He also practiced his Feline Karate moves. Although he had earned the Yellow Scarf, he was going to begin practicing and training for the coveted Black Scarf, 3rd degree – the very highest level possible in Feline Karate – very soon.

Kitty Wappis also practiced playing his three-ba! musical instrument. Have you heard of a three-ba! musical instrument? It IS very rare! Kitty Wappis had taught himself to play the three-ba! musical instrument. Have you ever heard of a One-ba? Or, perhaps, have you seen a Four-ba? You must have heard, and seen, the Two-ba(TUBA), right?

Kitty Wappis usually ate his breakfast V-E-R-Y slowly. That way the sun had a chance to warm his cushion for his mid-morning catnap. The cushion was in his special bridge with lots of windows. Sometimes, he climbed to his cushion v e r y slowly, too. This morning the sun was extra bright so his cushion should be almost warm by now.

Kitty Wappis climbed to his cushion and stretched out his little toe to test the temperature of his cushion. HMMmmm, JUST RIGHT! Kitty Wappis tiptoed onto his cushion, turned around twice, and plopped down right smack in the middle of the sunbeam! Kitty Wappis curled into a ball, tucked his nose under his tail, closed his eyes… decided to dream about the building project… and went instantly asleep. Do you fall asleep that fast?

This afternoon, after his long mid-morning catnap, Kitty Wappis was supposed to finish designing the new solar panels for the new addition onto the house owned by Mr. Alexander P. Frockmorton III. This is where Kitty Wappis lived. Actually, he lived in the middle between the two houses. The taller house was owned by Mr. Alexander P. Frockmorton III and the smaller house was owned by Mr. J. Cobb (G.O.E.). These were the two best friends of Kitty Wappis. Kitty Wappis lived in the connecting bridge between the two houses that was built especially for Kitty Wappis. Mr. J. Cobb (G.O.E.) was a retired master wood craftsman and he built the special bridge. It had to be very special because Kitty Wappis was a very special and strange kitty cat. The bridge had to be extra wide and extra high because Kitty Wappis could walk upright on his hind feet with his tail swishing back and forth and from side to side. Sometimes, when he walked upright, his upper torso would lean. Sometimes, he would LEAN to the right. Sometimes, he would LEAN to the left. Sometimes, when his tail was on the same side he was leaning, one would think that he would just fall over....but, he never did!

Kitty Wappis was a very good dreamer, too. Kitty Wappis dreamed about the solar panels he must design for the room addition for Mr. Alexander P. Frockmorton III. He dreamed about the different materials. He dreamed about the measurements. He dreamed about the proper angles and other features. Then, he dreamed that his job was done! Are you a good dreamer, too?

This evening all the plans were to be double checked. Kitty Wappis helped Mr. Alexander P. Frockmorton III and Mr. J. Cobb (G.O.E.) check all the schedules and the plans for the workmen to begin working on in the morning. Everything seemed ready to start the building project!

When the workmen came they all had assigned tasks. The digging people dug. The concrete people concreted. The electricians electrified. The plumbers plumbed! The heating and cooling people heated and cooled...and they installed the solar panels! The painters painted. The carpenters hammered and sawed!

Before they knew it, the job was completed! Everyone was very proud of their work. They all had a little celebration party. Mr. Alexander P. Frockmorton III was very proud of his new room. Mr. J. Cobb (G.O.E.) was very proud of his job, too! Kitty Wappis was very proud of his design of the solar panels! Kitty Wappis was so proud that he strutted down the hallway, smiling at everyone!

The workmen had never seen a kitty cat like Kitty Wappis. They had never seen a kitty cat that could read the newspaper, or do crossword puzzles, or even design solar panels! They certainly had never seen a kitty cat that could walk upright on his hind feet with his tail swishing back and forth and from side to side; Or a kitty cat that sometimes leaned to the right or leaned to the left; Or a kitty cat that almost fell over……but, never did!

Are you sure that you have never seen a kitty cat smile? Have you ever seen a kitty cat walk upright on his hind feet……………..?

The end of another purr-fect adventure.

List all of the ways that you save energy in your home.

Episode Eight: THE CIRCUS

Kitty Wappis was enjoying himself in front of the fireplace in the newly added room. This house was owned by Mr. Alexander P. Frockmorton III. He was one of the very best friends of Kitty Wappis. The other best friend was Mr. J. Cobb (G.O.E.). He always liked to use the initials "G.O.E." after his name. It meant that he was retired from working and the letters meant "Gentleman Of Ease". Mr. J. Cobb (G.O.E.) had built the special bridge – with lots of windows – that connected the two houses of his two very best friends.

The glowing embers in the fireplace made the room extra cozy today! Kitty Wappis was very comfortable in the large leather chair with the overstuffed pillows. He was reading the Sunday newspaper. Kitty Wappis liked the Sunday newspaper because it was extra thick. It had the comic sections and the special event sections. It also had a very big crossword puzzle section!

Kitty Wappis was on the very edge of falling asleep. His eyelids felt very heavy and were more than half closed. His breathing was very slow. His whiskers were beginning to droop. He may have even started to snore! Kitty Wappis was starting to drop his head when one eye caught sight of a particular advertisement in the newspaper!

The FILUSTER FELINE FLYING CIRCUS was coming to town! The FILUSTER FELINE FLYING CIRCUS was announcing the star of the BIG TOP (the main circus tent)! The star of the show is MISS MOR-GAN WAPPIS!! What a surprise to Kitty Wappis! His sister was the star of the show! Kitty Wappis was suddenly very awake! He read the entire newspaper article! It said that MISS MOR-GAN only performed with the FILUSTER FELINE FLYING CIRCUS once a year! She is usually dancing the Ballet or climbing mountains in far-off lands! She walks the high wire, does acrobatics and some trapeze acts, too! The FILUSTER FELINE FLYING CIRCUS will only be visiting this area for two days!

The telephone rang in the hallway downstairs. It was next to the big old Grandfather clock but too far for Kitty Wappis to answer it before the answering machine recorded the call. WHAT A COINCIDENCE! It was MISS MOR-GAN calling for Kitty Wappis! Kitty Wappis contacted his sister and they talked for a long time. MISS MOR-GAN wanted Kitty Wappis to come visit her and watch the circus performance. She said that she had tickets for him and his two very best friends!

That evening, at dinner with his two very best friends, Kitty Wappis showed them the newspaper article. He told them that he had talked to his sister and she had tickets for him.......and he could bring two friends. Who could they be?

Mr. J. Cobb (G.O.E.) looked at Kitty Wappis.
Mr. Alexander P. Frockmorton III looked at Kitty Wappis.
Mr. J. Cobb (G.O.E.) looked at Mr. Alexander P. Frockmorton III.

Kitty Wappis looked at both of his two very best friends and told them he wanted them to go with him to see the circus and his sister!

The trio set out to see the FILUSTER FELINE FLYING CIRCUS and MISS MOR-GAN WAPPIS, the star of the show! Mr. Alexander P. Frockmorton III was wearing his plaid suit over his bright yellow vest...and carried a walking stick! Mr. J. Cobb (G.O.E.) had a nice new suit...and a bowler hat! Kitty Wappis looked very handsome, too. He had a nice grooming and his nails and whiskers were nicely trimmed. He carried a bouquet of flowers for his sister! Wasn't that a nice thing to do?

They were quite a sight to see!

Kitty Wappis was a very strange kitty cat. Kitty Wappis could walk upright with his tail swishing back and forth and from side to side… and carrying a bouquet of flowers! Sometimes, when he walked upright, his upper torso would lean. Sometimes, he would LEAN to the right…and the bouquet of flowers would almost touch the ground! Sometimes, he would LEAN to the left….and the bouquet of flowers would almost touch the ground on that side! Sometimes, when his tail was on the same side he was leaning, one would think that he would just fall over (or, at least the flowers would!)…..but, he (and the flowers) never did!

Mr. J. Cobb (G.O.E.), Mr. Alexander P. Frockmorton III, and Kitty Wappis watched the entire circus acts. MISS MOR-GAN was absolutely outstanding! She received many standing ovations! She was truly the STAR OF THE SHOW!! Kitty Wappis was very proud of his sister!

Everyone met after the show to say their good-byes. MISS MOR-GAN was very happy that Kitty Wappis could come and thanked him for the beautiful bouquet of flowers. She was very happy that Mr. J .Cobb (G.O.E.) and Mr. Alexander P. Frockmorton III were there, too! MISS MOR-GAN signed all their programs and kissed Kitty Wappis good-bye!

Kitty Wappis was smiling all the way home! Have you ever seen a kitty cat smile?)

The end of another purr-fect adventure.

Draw a picture of your favorite circus animals.

Episode Nine: THE MOVIE STAR

This morning Kitty Wappis was practicing his Feline Karate moves. He studied very hard because he wanted to test for the coveted Black Scarf, 3rd degree – the very highest level possible in Feline Karate! He needed to be perfect in all the disciplined movements as the testing date would be here very soon! Kitty Wappis was watching a videotape on the television describing the proper form and moves he must be able to do. He practiced all the different maneuvers intently!

Kitty Wappis stopped to rest and switched the television back to the regular channels. Something caught the corner of his eye……and his ears perked up, too! Then, the television got his full attention!

There, right in front of his face, on the full screen of the television was his sister! Miss Jor-Dan, the famous Feline movie star and model! (Have you ever heard of Miss Jor-Dan?) She was starring in a new movie and it was making its premier showing right here in this city! Miss Jor-Dan was making a rare appearance on stage before the movie began! Miss Jor-Dan Wappis! WOW! Kitty Wappis was very excited to see his sister on the television! He decided that he MUST go!

Just as Kitty Wappis reached for the telephone, it rang! (Has that ever happened to you?) It was Miss Jor-Dan! She wanted to talk to Kitty Wappis about coming to see her. She was only here in the city for the one day to help promote the movie. She certainly wanted to see her brother, too!

Kitty Wappis was excited to talk to his sister! They hadn't spoken to each other for a long time! They talked a long time. Kitty Wappis agreed to meet his sister at the movie theater. Kitty Wappis shouldn't be late because Miss Jor-Dan had to give a little speech before the movie started.

Kitty Wappis combed his hair, checked his nails, and brushed his teeth. He then made arrangements for a florist to deliver some flowers to Miss Jor-Dan. Wasn't that a nice thing to do?

He remembered that the last time he saw his sister was at a Feline Karate testing station. Kitty Wappis was testing for the Yellow Scarf! It seemed like such a long time ago!

Kitty Wappis fetched his umbrella. (It looked like it could rain any minute!). Kitty Wappis left his house and used the sidewalk. Kitty Wappis was quite a sight to see! Have you ever seen a kitty cat carrying an umbrella? Kitty Wappis was a very strange kitty cat!

Kitty Wappis could walk upright on his hind feet with his tail swishing back and forth and from side to side. Sometimes, when he walked upright, his upper torso would lean. Sometimes, he would LEAN to the right. Sometimes, he would LEAN to the left. Sometimes, when his tail was on the same side he was leaning, one would think that he would just fall over...but, he never did!

Kitty Wappis arrived at the movie theater and located his sister. They were very excited to see each other! They talked right up to the very last minute. Miss Jor-Dan had to give a little speech before the movie began. She gave Kitty Wappis a ticket for a seat in the very first row in the balcony section – the very best seat in the theater! The movie theater was "STANDING ROOM ONLY"...every seat was taken! The theater was overflowing with Miss Jor-Dan movie fans!

Everyone enjoyed the movie immensely! There were many "BRAVOS" and much applauding! The audience had loved every minute of the movie! WHAT A TERRIFIC ACTRESS! Kitty Wappis decided that he would never miss another one of Miss Jor-Dan's movies!

Kitty Wappis met his sister after the movie. She introduced him to so many actors, directors, stage hands, and producers that he was getting dizzy! Miss Jor-Dan told Kitty Wappis that her director wanted to make a movie about Kitty Wappis. They had never seen a kitty cat that could walk upright, or read books, or do jigsaw puzzles lickety split, or do crossword puzzles, or do Feline Karate moves, or even play a three-ba! musical instrument! (Have you ever heard of a three- ba! musical instrument? It IS very rare!)

Kitty Wappis was AWESTRUCK! A movie about himself!!?? Kitty Wappis didn't know exactly what to say! Kitty Wappis had to sit down to think about this proposal!

Kitty Wappis WAS very happy with his life.
Kitty Wappis HAS two houses connected with his special bridge with lots of windows.
Kitty Wappis HAS a cushion warmed every day by the sun
Kitty Wappis HAS lots of friends.
Kitty Wappis COULD NOT think of himself as a movie star.
Kitty Wappis DID NOT think the movie star life style was for him.

Kitty Wappis told his sister, Miss Jor-Dan, that he really liked his life the way it was and just didn't want to change it. Kitty Wappis thanked everyone for the nice offer!

Kitty Wappis was very proud of his sister! He told her he missed her and promised to watch every movie she made!

Kitty Wappis was so proud of his sister that he did a little dance on the way home. Are you sure you haven't EVER seen a kitty cat dancing on the sidewalk or carrying an umbrella?

As he danced his way home, Kitty Wappis was smiling, too! Have you ever seen a kitty cat smile?

The end of another purr-fect adventure.

Episode Ten: THE ACCIDENT

Kitty Wappis and Mr. Alexander P. Frockmorton III were enjoying the fireplace and discussing some science projects. Mr. Alexander P. Frockmorton III was a very best friend of Kitty Wappis. The other best friend was Mr. J. Cobb (G.O.E.). Kitty Wappis had a special bridge – with lots of windows – between their two houses.

The library was very quiet except for the occasional snapping of the wood on the fire. Kitty Wappis noticed it first. There seemed to be a slight rustling noise in the ceiling. Kitty Wappis had much better hearing than Mr. Alexander P. Frockmorton III, but he noticed it, too! It was late in the evening and very close to bedtime so they agreed to investigate this noise the next day. Mr. Alexander P. Frockmorton III said that he had never been up there. Whatever is up there was left behind by the former owners. Kitty Wappis thought that it could be fun and interesting. There could be some hidden treasures, or some important documents, or….. just nothing!

Mr. Alexander P. Frockmorton III told Kitty Wappis that the door to the attic space had been locked for years. He would look for the key in the morning.

As soon as breakfast was over Kitty Wappis and Mr. Alexander P. Frockmorton III found the key.

When they unlocked the old door, it creaked awfully loud! (almost as if it was telling them not to go up there!). They pried the door open as far as they could. It was a very narrow door – much too narrow for Mr. Alexander P. Frockmorton III. Kitty Wappis would have to go up the fragile looking ladder by himself! There were no electric lights up there so Kitty Wappis would have to rely on his good eyesight (because kitty cats can see in the dark, you know) and the flashlight.

The ladder was very dusty. It made Kitty Wappis sneeze! (You must have heard and seen a kitty cat sneeze, right?). Kitty Wappis would climb up one step (the steps were very far apart!) and.....AHHCHOO! Kitty Wappis would climb up the next step and.....AHHHHCCHHOOO! Kitty Wappis had ten more steps to climb.....AHHCHOO....AHHCHOO....AHHCHOO....AHHCHOO

...AHHCHOO!...AHHCHOO!...AHHCHOO!....AHHCHOO!.... AHHCHOO!...AHHCHOO!

Now his nose was running and his eyes had tears in them!

Kitty Wappis turned on the flashlight. It created some very scary shadows! Kitty Wappis had very good eyesight – when he wasn't sneezing! He climbed into the attic and looked around. He saw lots of boxes and some old paintings in very ornate frames. He saw an antique spinning wheel (Do you what that is?) and, he saw a lot of spider webs!

Kitty Wappis was pushing a large spider web out of his way when his foot slipped. Kitty Wappis fell backwards! The flashlight flew out of his hand and crashed nearby! Kitty Wappis fell onto a large cardboard box (luckily!) and the side of the box tore open! What seemed to be a bowling ball rumbled across the floor of the attic toward the ladder. It rumbled toward Mr. Alexander P. Frockmorton III! It barely missed him! Kitty Wappis turned just in time to see another box fall toward him. Kitty Wappis jumped out of the way.....but, the wrong way!

Kitty Wappis fell against the ladder and twisted and bounced and turned and bounced again off of every step of the ladder! Kitty Wappis almost landed on the bowling ball! Mr. Alexander P. Frockmorton III caught Kitty Wappis just in the very last second but............Kitty Wappis had a cut over his eyebrow! Kitty

Wappis had a cut on the back of his head! Kitty Wappis had a very swollen ankle on his hind foot! To say the least, Kitty Wappis was very shaken, too!

Mr. Alexander P. Frockmorton III grabbed a pillow, a blanket, and some bandages. He carried Kitty Wappis quickly downstairs and applied an ice pack to the swollen ankle. He grabbed the car keys, placed Kitty Wappis in the special seat, and raced to the animal hospital!

The car's horn blared and the tires squealed as Mr. Alexander P. Frockmorton III arrived at the animal hospital emergency entrance. The attendants placed Kitty Wappis on a stretcher and rushed him inside! Kitty Wappis had the best of care! His cuts were bandaged and an X-ray was taken of his ankle. Luckily, there were no broken bones! After the swelling went down in a few days, the doctor wanted to put a small walking cast on the foot and ankle.

The doctor told him he was very lucky to have such a friend to look after him. The doctor didn't know that Kitty Wappis could, sometimes, walk upright.... but not for a few days! In a few short weeks, the ankle should be fine again.

Kitty Wappis was a very smart kitty cat. Kitty Wappis also was a very strange kitty cat. Kitty Wappis could walk upright on his hind feet with his tail swishing back and forth and from side to side. Sometimes, when he walked upright, his upper torso would lean. Sometimes, he would LEAN to the right. Sometimes, he would LEAN to the left. Sometimes, when his tail was on the same side he was leaning, one would think that he would just fall over.....but, he never did!

Kitty Wappis was discharged from the animal hospital into the good care of Mr. Alexander P. Frockmorton III. Kitty Wappis was a very lucky kitty cat! Kitty Wappis even managed to smile on the way home. Have you ever seen a kitty cat smile?

The end of another purr-fect adventure.

Unscramble the words below to find some items hidden in the attic.

ICURETPS

____

SLODL

____

DARIO

____

NURKT

____

SKOBO

____

SREDPIS

____

MALP

____

BLETA

____

Answers are on page 112

Episode 11: THE MARCHING BAND

Kitty Wappis awoke from his mid-morning catnap. The sunshine – in his special bridge with lots of windows – had been so inviting that he couldn't resist!

Kitty Wappis, just yesterday as a matter of fact, was fitted with a walking cast on his hind foot. Although all of his bruises and cuts from his fall in the attic had mostly healed, his ankle needed a bit more support to heal properly. The walking cast limited his ability to walk upright so Kitty Wappis decided to spend some time with the computer. Kitty Wappis and one of his very best friends, Mr. Alexander P. Frockmorton III, had learned how to use the new computer only a few months ago. Mr. Alexander P. Frockmorton III was very glad he had the technicians install it, too! This new one was very much easier to use! This would be a great time for Kitty Wappis to catch up on all his messages. He wanted to work on a special project, too.

Kitty Wappis wanted to create an animal marching band to participate in the many parades the city had for different events. It seemed like there was a parade every week! The parades had fire trucks and floats, and, of course, the Mayor was always there, and members of the city council, and sometimes, even the Governor came to march, too.

Kitty Wappis contacted the local branch of the YKCA ("Young Kitty Cat Association") to see if it would be possible to have some animals, not just the kitty cats, represented in the city parades.

Would it be possible, also, to have the animals play musical instruments, too? Have you ever seen any animals in the city parades? Have you seen any animals playing musical instruments in the city parades? Some animals, not just the kitty cats, were very talented musicians!

As a matter of fact, Kitty Wappis was teaching himself to play the three-ba! musical instrument. Have you ever heard of a three-ba! musical instrument? It IS very rare! Have you ever heard of the One-ba!, or the Four-ba!? You must have heard of the Two-ba! (Tuba), right?

The three-ba! musical instrument sounded more like… wellll, kind-of…. wellll, sort-of….well, maybe a bit softer sounding…..welll, it is hard to describe…. but, it is lot smaller! It is considered a brass instrument. (Remember, it is very rare!)

Kitty Wappis was a very smart kitty cat. Also, Kitty Wappis was a very strange kitty cat. Kitty Wappis could walk upright on his hind feet (when he didn't have a walking cast on his hind foot!) with his tail swishing back and forth and from side to side. Sometimes, when he walked upright, his upper torso would lean. Sometimes he would LEAN to the right. Sometimes, he would LEAN to the left. Sometimes, when his tail was on the same side he was leaning, one would think that he would just fall over……but, he never did!

Although Kitty Wappis still had to wear the walking cast, he practiced playing his three-ba! musical instrument. He would practice carrying it correctly while reading the music sheets. Actually, he used the clicking noise from the walking cast to help with the rhythm! Click went the walking cast against the floor and toot went the three-ba!... and LEAN to the right! Click went the walking cast, toot went the three-ba!... and LEAN to the left! Kitty Wappis was quite a sight to see!

Kitty Wappis talked with lots of his friends about the marching band idea. All his friends thought it was a terrific idea and some even wanted to learn how to play different musical instruments! It would require many, many practice sessions but everyone agreed to try!

Many, many animals came to practice. There were many different musical instruments.

There were drums! There were cymbals! There were trumpets! There were flutes! There was even a saxophone and one sliding trombone! (Don't stand too close to the sliding trombone!). Oh yes, there was one three-ba! musical instrument too! (Who played that?)

Mr. Alexander P. Frockmorton III was the conductor! Mr. J. Cobb (G.O.E.) [The other very best friend of Kitty Wappis] played a trumpet and helped, too!

Kitty Wappis invited the city mayor and the city council members to the final practice. This would be their best performance because all the animals wanted to march and play their musical instruments in the parades!

Kitty Wappis tapped his walking cast against the floor and blew a whistle. Mr. Alexander P. Frockmorton III lifted his baton to direct the band. CLICK! CLICK! CLICK! 1! And 2! And 3! And the Animal Marching Band played The National Anthem! CLICK! CLICK! CLICK! went the tapping from the walking cast and Mr. Alexander P. Frockmorton III lifted his baton again! This time the animals marched and played at the same time! They played and marched very well!

The city Mayor and the Council members were very impressed! The Mayor called for a Proclamation declaring the official acceptance of the animal marching band into all the city parades! HOORAY TO ALL THE MEMBERS OF THE MARCHING BAND!

Kitty Wappis, Mr. J. Cobb (G.O.E.), and Mr. Alexander P. Frockmorton III were very proud of the fine animal band!

Kitty Wappis was smiling from ear to ear. Have you ever seen a kitty cat smile?

The end of another purr-fect adventure.

The Adventures

Episode 12: THE MAGIC SHOW

Kitty Wappis awoke abruptly from his afternoon catnap. He had been dreaming about big trucks, or airplanes, or something that made lots of noise. He usually remembered his dreams but this catnap ended too fast! But, he soon found out what made the loud noise! It was THUNDER! The afternoon sunshine that warmed his cushion – in his special bridge with lots of windows – had disappeared behind a large dark cloud. Soon there was lightning flashes in the distance.

Kitty Wappis left the comfort of his cushion and the special bridge. He thought that the safest place to be was the library that belonged to one of his very best friends. Kitty Wappis had TWO very best friends that lived next to one another. The special bridge – with lots of windows – connected the two houses. The taller house belonged to Mr. Alexander P. Frockmorton III and the other house belonged to Mr. J. Cobb (G.O.E.). Mr. J. Cobb always liked to use those letters (G.O.E.) because they meant "Gentleman Of Ease". He wanted everyone to know that he was retired from working.

Kitty Wappis could choose from many books to read until the storm passed. Kitty Wappis stretched way up on his very tippy toes of his hind feet to reach a book on the top shelf. His front foot didn't quite reach the book, but his whiskers did! Kitty Wappis carefully slid the book toward him by his two longest whiskers when…

…KKKAAAABBOOOOOMMMM went the thunder!

LO and BEHOLD! HOLY COW! (and cats, too!) and TWO BIG MEOWS!

THE ENTIRE HOUSE SHOOK!!

Kitty Wappis fell to the floor. Some of the books fell completely off the shelves, too. Luckily, Kitty Wappis wasn't injured by any falling books. The lights went out and it became very dark in the library. Kitty Wappis was a kitty cat and everyone knows that kitty cats can see in the dark. Right? Kitty Wappis looked at all the fallen books. The closest one to him was a book about magic and magicians. Kitty Wappis put that book aside until the lights came back on. It would certainly be easier to read then!

The thunderstorm finally left and all the power was restored. Kitty Wappis plopped himself into the big leather chair in front of the fireplace and opened the book about magic and magicians. Kitty Wappis enjoyed this book very much! There were stories about magic that were over 500 years old! He read almost the entire book! Near the end of the book were stories and pictures on how to do some magic. Kitty Wappis found some string and tried some magic as he read more and more. WOW! THIS WAS FASCINATING! Kitty Wappis found a deck of ordinary playing cards and followed some more instructions. WOW! THIS MAGIC IS FUN! Kitty Wappis found some coins and tried another magic trick and....CAN YOU GUESS WHAT HAPPENED?...

....he could make the coins disappear and reappear, too.

Kitty Wappis put the fallen books back on the top shelf. This time he used the ladder to be safe! He found some other books on magic and brought these down to read.

Kitty Wappis climbed back into that big leather chair in front of the fireplace. He fluffed the pillow behind his back and opened the second book. This book told how to perform more magic tricks. Kitty Wappis couldn't wait to try some of these tricks after dinner. Kitty Wappis opened the third book and found more instructions and directions. He didn't really want to pull a rabbit out of a hat, but he learned how to do it!

That evening, after dinner, Kitty Wappis was discussing the magic books with

Mr. Alexander P. Frockmorton III. Kitty Wappis was very pleased with himself for learning some magic tricks. Mr. Alexander P. Frockmorton III showed Kitty Wappis some magic tricks that he could do! Then, they would take turns doing magic tricks! It was fun!

The next day Kitty Wappis invited Mr. O. and his twin cats, Sherlock and Spurlock, and KoKo, Samantha and Jake, and even Mr. J. Cobb (G.O.E.), to the library to surprise them with the magic he had learned last night.

Kitty Wappis was a very smart kitty cat.....although he was a bit strange, too. Kitty Wappis could walk upright on his hind feet with his tail swishing back and forth and from side to side. Sometimes, when he walked upright, his upper torso would lean. Sometimes, he would LEAN to the right. Sometimes, he would LEAN to the left. Sometimes, when his tail was on the same side he was leaning, one would think that he would just fall over......but, he never did!

Kitty Wappis surprised his friends with his magic. He plucked a coin from Samantha's ear. He named the playing card that Jake had hidden back into the deck. He made some things disappear, then reappear! They all loved his magic! They all congratulated Kitty Wappis! They all had an enjoyable visit.

Kitty Wappis smiled all the way to his special bridge! Have you ever seen a kitty cat smile?

The end of another purr-fect adventure.

STICKY
WICKET
ANIMAL CLINIC
S.W.I.S.H

Episode 13: THE CLINIC DREAM

Kitty Wappis was being examined by his veterinarian, Dr. Paul. It was time for his annual physical examination and vaccinations. Kitty Wappis wanted to stay as healthy as possible. You, too?

Dr. Paul explained that this vaccination could make Kitty Wappis very sleepy and quite possibly cause some bad dreams. Everything would return to normal in a couple of days. He didn't want Kitty Wappis to worry!

Kitty Wappis got home just in time. He was feeling very sleepy. Usually, he waits until his cushion in his special bridge – with lots of windows – is warmed by the sun before he takes his mid-morning catnap. Hopefully, the cushion is warm because Kitty Wappis was having a hard time staying awake to climb that far. Kitty Wappis stretched out his little toe to test the temperature of his cushion. He was so tired now that the temperature really didn't matter! He didn't even tiptoe onto his cushion but sort-of just plopped on the edge of it and rolled in! He barely had time to curl into a ball or tuck his nose under his tail before his eyes closed! He was asleep even before his nose touched his tail!

Kitty Wappis dreamed and dreamed. He dreamed about being an astronaut. Can you imagine a kitty cat astronaut? Kitty Wappis dreamed about being a soccer star and scoring the winning goal! A kitty cat soccer player!!?? Kitty Wappis dreamed about being an ocean liner ship's captain! A kitty cat ship captain!!?? Kitty Wappis was having some strange dreams! Do you ever have strange dreams like this?

Kitty Wappis dreamed he could help other animals. This was a very nice dream so he thought he should continue with this one! He dreamed of several ways that he could help other animals. He must dream this very carefully and work out all the details!

He dreamed about his childhood back in Sticky Wicket where he was born. He dreamed of his brothers and sisters and all of his friends. He dreamed of all the friends at his school, too. He had many friends at The Sticky Wicket Purr-fect KittyGarden School. THAT'S IT!

This would be the perfect thing! Kitty Wappis could build a clinic for all the animals in Sticky Wicket......or animals from anywhere! Many people come to Sticky Wicket to adopt different animals so the animals must be healthy! Kitty Wappis smiled in his dreams. (Have you ever seen a kitty cat smile?) Kitty Wappis must now dream about this needed clinic. How would it get built?

How much would it cost? Who would be the staff? There were many, many, questions he dreamed about, for sure!

Kitty Wappis dreamed about his brothers and sisters. He even dreamed about Titus B! - the famous Feline rock band star! Kitty Wappis had too many friends to list them all in his dream! WAIT! MAYBE THAT'S THE ANSWER! YES! Kitty Wappis could certainly help the animals this way!

Kitty Wappis was so excited about this project that he woke up! He immediately wrote down all of his ideas so he would not forget any detail! Kitty Wappis was a very smart kitty cat. Kitty Wappis could read the newspaper...and do the crossword puzzle. He could do jigsaw puzzles lickety split! He practiced Feline Karate and taught himself to play the three-ba! musical instrument! (Have you heard of the three-ba! musical instrument. It IS very rare! Have you heard of the One- ba, or the Four-ba? You must have heard of the Two-ba(TUBA), right?)

Kitty Wappis was a very strange kitty cat. Kitty Wappis could walk upright on his hind feet with his tail swishing back and forth and from side to side.

Sometimes, when he walked upright, his upper torso would lean. Sometimes, he would LEAN to the right. Sometimes, he would LEAN to the left. Sometimes, when his tail was on the same side he was leaning, one would think that he would just fall over...but, he never did!

Kitty Wappis contacted his famous sister, Miss Jor-Dan. She was a famous Feline movie star and model. Kitty Wappis contacted his other sister, too! She was a famous Feline Ballet star, mountain climber, and part-time acrobat! (Have you ever heard of Miss Mor-Gan?) Kitty Wappis contacted his friend Titus B!, the famous Feline rock star! Kitty Wappis contacted everyone he could possibly think of! He even told his two very best friends about this project! Mr. Alexander P. Frockmorton III thought it was a splendid idea! After all, it was Mr. Alexander P. Frockmorton III that had adopted Kitty Wappis in Sticky Wicket some time ago! Mr. J. Cobb (G.O.E.) agreed also, and even offered to help!

THE DREAM WAS BECOMING A REALITY!

The necessary funds were raised and the construction had begun....thanks to all of the friends of Kitty Wappis...and all their friends.....and the friends of friends.....and friends of more friends....and on and on and on!

Soon the new clinic was finished in Sticky Wicket! Dr. Paul was the new director!

Also, there was a second building. It was a special building for preventive medicine for the animals. Its official name was the STICKY WICKET INSTITUTE FOR SAFETY AND HEALTH. It was simply called by its nickname of "SWISH"!

Everyone was very proud of the new buildings! Kitty Wappis was especially proud of all his friends! Kitty Wappis always smiled when he thought of the new animal clinic in Sticky Wicket! (Are you sure you haven't seen a kitty cat smile?)

The end of another purr-fect adventure.

Episode 14: TWO HEROES

Kitty Wappis awoke from his mid-morning catnap very refreshed. He had worked hard this morning after watching the moon set. He did some jigsaw puzzles lickety split, read the morning newspaper, and did the crossword puzzle, too! Just before breakfast, he practiced some Feline Karate maneuvers because he always wanted to stay mentally and physically fit. Kitty Wappis had earned his Yellow Scarf in Feline Karate and soon will begin special training to earn the coveted Black Scarf, 3rd degree – the highest level possible!

Kitty Wappis lived with his two very best friends; Mr. Alexander P. Frockmorton III and Mr. J. Cobb (G.O.E.) [Mr. J. Cobb always used (G.O.E) after his name because he wanted everyone to know that he was retired from working full time. The letters meant "Gentleman Of Ease"]. Mr. Alexander P. Frockmorton III lived in the taller house and Mr. J. Cobb (G.O.E.) lived in the house next door. Mr. J. Cobb (G.O.E.) had built the special bridge for Kitty Wappis that connected the two houses. The bridge had to be very special. It had to be just the right width and just the right height and had to have lots of windows. Kitty Wappis was a very strange kitty cat and the bridge had to be very, very, special because Kitty Wappis could walk upright on his hind feet with his tail swishing back and forth and from side to side. Sometimes, when he walked upright, his upper torso would lean. Sometimes, he would LEAN to the right. Sometimes, he would LEAN to the left. Sometimes, when his tail was on the same side he was leaning, one would think that he would just fall over.....but, he never did!

Kitty Wappis and Mr. J. Cobb (G.O.E.) were going to the park this afternoon. Perhaps they might see Mr. O. and his twin cats, Sherlock and Spurlock. Those twin cats always had some important news for Kitty Wappis.

When they arrived at the park, Mr. O. and his twin cats, Sherlock and Spurlock were at the water fountain! As usual, the twin cats were full of information! This time it really WAS important. They told Kitty Wappis about the huge ANNUAL FELINE CONFERENCE. This was the first time it was being held in this area. There were many classes, seminars, and conferences. It WAS NOT to be missed! Also, for the little kittens – and maybe – those a bit older – there was to be a KITTY KARNIVAL with rides and games! The twin cats were excited and were planning to attend! They had already registered for some of the classes!

After returning home, Kitty Wappis and Mr. J. Cobb (G.O.E.) looked for information about the ANNUAL FELINE CONFERENCE. There were some classes and seminars that seemed very interesting. They both signed up for the same class! Then they signed up for another class in the afternoon! The first class met at 10 am. They could eat lunch after the class at the KITTY KARNIVAL and watch the kittens on the rides until the afternoon class would begin!

Kitty Wappis wore his Yellow Scarf and Mr. J. Cobb (G.O.E.) wore a bright red cap so they could find each other in the large crowd!

When their early morning class ended, they went to the KITTY KARNIVAL to watch the little kittens. There were many different rides! There was the tea cup spinning ride, the KITTY roller coaster, and the BIG WHEEL RIDE. It went very high and the kittens sat inside a caged gondola so they wouldn't fall out when it spun and turned!

SUDDENLY THERE WAS A LOUD SCREAM!

One of the swinging, turning, caged gondolas – with little kittens in it – had broken one of its cables! The caged gondola was dangling by only the upper cable and a very, very narrow bar! It was hanging over a water pond and the rescue ladders wouldn't be able to reach that far!

Kitty Wappis immediately decided what needed to be done! He climbed over the security fence and into the inside framework of the BIG WHEEL RIDE! The crowd gasped as he climbed higher and higher! Kitty Wappis reached the upper cable assembly. Because Kitty Wappis sometimes walked upright on his hind feet, he stood on the very, very, narrow bar. He walked upright on that narrow bar balancing with his whiskers until he reached the upper cabling! He undid the cage door and lifted the first little kitten out. Mr. J. Cobb (G.O.E.) had found some rope and threw one end to Kitty Wappis. Kitty Wappis made a sling from his Yellow Scarf and tied the first little kitten inside it. Then he tied the sling over the rope and slid the Yellow Scarf sling down to Mr. J. Cobb (G.O.E.).

The first little kitten was saved! The rope was tossed to Kitty Wappis again and the other little kitten was saved the same way! The crowd gasped, then applauded. The crowd said that Kitty Wappis and Mr. J. Cobb (G.O.E.) were heroes for saving the little kittens!

Mr. J. Cobb (G.O.E.) and Kitty Wappis decided to miss the afternoon class and went home. Mr. J. Cobb (G.O.E.) was very proud of Kitty Wappis and Kitty Wappis was very proud of Mr. J. Cobb (G.O.E.)!

Kitty Wappis smiled all the way home! Have you ever seen a kitty cat smile?

The end of another purr-fect adventure.

Episode 15: ALL THE BERRIES

Kitty Wappis awoke from his midmorning catnap with a start! It seemed as though he didn't sleep very long. He remembered tiptoeing onto his sun-warmed cushion - in his special bridge with lots of windows - tucking his nose under his tail, and closing his eyes, but he didn't remember any dreams. Kitty Wappis was a very good dreamer, too! Are you? Then he discovered why!

LO and BEHOLD! HOLY COW! (and cats, too!) and TWO BIG MEOWS!

THE JACKHAMMERS STARTED!! What a noise! The road crews were hard at work ….and almost directly under the special bridge that connected the two houses of his two very best friends: Mr. Alexander P. Frockmorton III and Mr. J. Cobb (G.O.E.). (Mr. J. Cobb always used G.O.E. after his name so everyone would know he was retired from working full time. The letters meant "Gentleman Of Ease").

Kitty Wappis tied a pillow over his ears and went down to the kitchen. Mr. Alexander P. Frockmorton III was already there just having some morning tea. He looked quite strange because he was wearing some ear muffs! The jackhammer noise and the heavy equipment noise were becoming unbearable!

While Kitty Wappis was drinking his tea, he peeked at the morning newspaper. Sometimes, when he was up very early watching the moon set, he liked to do the crossword puzzles. It was much too noisy today! As he turned a page of the newspaper, a certain advertisement caught his eye. PICK YOUR OWN BERRIES! Kitty Wappis became very curious. (Aren't all kitty cats curious?) PICK

CHOKECHERRIES, CURRANTS (Both red and black!), and ELDERBERRIES! SOME RASPBERRIES ARE READY, TOO!! Well, Kitty Wappis knew what raspberries were but he had never heard of all those others! Have you? Kitty Wappis pointed out the advertisement to Mr. Alexander P. Frockmorton III. He seemed very intrigued, too! They both looked at each. Then, they both looked outside. Then they pointed to their ears. LET'S GO PICK BERRIES!!

They collected some baskets and buckets and loaded the car. Both of them wanted to know about the strange berries!

The big black automobile finally arrived at the berry picking farm. It was quite a distance from the city – and all that road construction noise! It was very quiet here except for an occasional tractor and some other berry pickers.

Kitty Wappis and Mr. Alexander P. Frockmorton III found the owners of the berry farm.

Mr. and Mrs. M. were very nice. They explained the different berries and even offered them a sample taste, too. Kitty Wappis thought the chokecherries were a bit sour and bitter – but all the other ones were delicious!

Mr. and Mrs. M. had never seen a kitty cat that could walk upright on his hind feet or pick berries...and they had a lot of different farm animals! Kitty Wappis was a very strange kitty cat.

Kitty Wappis could walk upright on his hind feet with his tail swishing back and forth and from side to side. Sometimes, when he walked upright, his upper torso would lean. Sometimes, he would LEAN to the right. Sometimes, he would LEAN to the left. Sometimes, when his tail was on the same side he was leaning, one would think that he would just fall over....but, he never did!

Kitty Wappis and Mr. Alexander P. Frockmorton III picked a lot of different berries.

(Perhaps they might have eaten a lot of berries, too!) Mr. Alexander P.

Frockmorton III actually mixed the elderberries with the two currants. He said the three different colors made them taste even better! Have you ever tried eating dark blue elderberries mixed with red and black currants? Mr. Alexander P. Frockmorton III thought that those three types of berries would be perfect on top of his kumquat pudding!

They must have picked a gazillion berries because all their baskets and buckets were full to the brim! Mr. and Mrs. M. told them how the clean them and freeze some for a later time. They might need gallons of ice cream (Kitty Wappis' favorite was purple ice cream!) and kumquat pudding for all these berries!

The sun was setting when the big black automobile entered the city. The road workers had left for the evening and the noise was gone. Kitty Wappis and Mr. Alexander P. Frockmorton III would have dinner then work on the berries. They couldn't wait for dessert!

They put their dinner in the oven to cook, set the timer, and started on the berries. Kitty Wappis sorted the berries and Mr. Alexander P. Frockmorton III cleaned and washed them. Of course after they were cleaned and washed, they had to be tasted again! Sort two, wash two, taste three! Sort three, wash three, taste four! Sort four, wash four, taste five! They soon discovered that the berry pile was getting smaller! This system was not quite working properly! They were almost finished with the berries when the oven timer told them their dinner was ready. For some reason, they weren't the least bit hungry! (Do you know why?) They even skipped their dessert.....for tonight!!

The end of another purr-fect adventure.

Episode 16: THE BIG TEST

Today was to be an exciting day for Kitty Wappis. This was the day for the BIG TEST. Today, Kitty Wappis will test for the coveted Black Scarf, 3rd degree in Feline Karate – the very highest level possible! He had practiced very hard! Luckily, he had help from his two very best friends; Mr. Alexander P. Frockmorton III and Mr. J. Cobb (G.O.E.). [Mr. J. Cobb always used the letters G.O.E. after his name. He was a retired wood master craftsman and he wanted everyone to know that he was retired from working full time. The letters meant "Gentleman Of Ease"]

Mr. Alexander P. Frockmorton III and Mr. J. Cobb (G.O.E.) had helped Kitty Wappis practice some of the very difficult Karate maneuvers. The SUPER-KITTY ESCAPE MANUEVER and the OUTWARD CLAW SELF-DEFENSE MOVE required much more time to learn. Kitty Wappis was already very proficient with most of the kicking moves. The hardest maneuver required much more flexibility and energy. It was the hardest one for Kitty Wappis to learn! Mr. Alexander P. Frockmorton III and Mr. J. Cobb (G.O.E.) spent a lot of time helping him practice. It was called THE QUAD-KICK, MID-AIR SPIN MANUEVER! It was a very difficult and dangerous move, indeed! Kitty Wappis must focus all of his energies to only one leg and foot at a time while high in the air as far as he could leap, arch his back in the STRIKE POSE, angle his tail in the ATTACK MODE, and be able to knock down four targets (one with each foot and leg) from four different pillars…ONE AT A TIME, and then land correctly in the proper stance (everyone knows that kitty cats always land on their feet, right?) and proceed with the next maneuver without any delay in movement! WHEW! A very dangerous and difficult move, indeed! (Remember, these are very difficult and dangerous move attempts. They take many, many hours of practice. Do not attempt any of these Feline Karate moves without the proper supervision and training!)

Can you imagine a kitty cat well trained enough to even attempt these moves in Feline Karate? Kitty Wappis was a very strange kitty cat. Kitty Wappis could walk upright on his hind feet with his tail swishing back and forth and from side to side. Sometimes, when he walked upright, his upper torso would lean. Sometimes, he would LEAN to the right. Sometimes, he would LEAN to the left. Sometimes, when his tail was on the same side he was leaning, one would think that he would just fall over...but, he never did!

The day arrived and Kitty Wappis was standing behind a large curtain. He was watching some other contestants compete for the Yellow Scarf. They were very good! Kitty Wappis remembered when he tested for the Yellow Scarf, too. It had been quite a while ago but he cherished that time in his life as very special. (Do you have any very special times you remember, too?) Kitty Wappis was especially thankful to his two very best friends for their support! (Do you remember their names?)

Mr. J. Cobb (G.O.E.) peeked out of the area behind the curtain to see the audience. All the seats were being filled! Mr. Alexander P. Frockmorton III and Mr. J. Cobb (G.O.E.) had planned a surprise for Kitty Wappis and they were delighted to see such a large audience! What a surprise!

Kitty Wappis looked out from behind the curtain again and.........

LO and BEHOLD! HOLY COW! (and cats, too!) and TWO BIG MEOWS!

There were some very special friends and relatives, too! There was Miss Jor-Dan! (She was a famous Feline movie star and model). There was Miss Mor-Gan! (She was a famous Feline Ballet star, mountain climber, and acrobat in The Filuster Feline Flying Circus!) These were actually his two sisters! Even Titus B! was here! (He was a famous Feline rock band musician and went to pre-school with Kitty Wappis way back in Sticky Wicket!) There was Uncle Jeff, too. He was in the Military and traveled all over the world. And Uncle Jason was here, too! What a surprise! Uncle Jason was an international Martial Arts instructor and examiner!

Kitty Wappis was certainly delighted to see so many of his friends and relatives! How did they know that he was testing today? It was time for Kitty Wappis to concentrate and focus on the task for today. He closed his eyes and focused his attention on each and every move he must do. He saw everything in his mind and pinpointed all his energies where they must go. He slowed his breathing and his heartbeats. KITTY WAPPIS WAS READY TO TEST FOR THE BLACK SCARF, 3rd DEGREE – THE VERY HIGHEST LEVEL!

Kitty Wappis went on the stage and bowed to the judges. He then began the difficult moves and maneuvers. He demonstrated the SUPER-KITTY ESCAPE and the FORWARD CLAW DEFENSE MOVES. He began the infamous QUAD-KICK – one of the hardest to do! He had practiced a long time with help from his two very best friends on this particular move. Kitty Wappis jumped high in the air, spun around once, and kicked his left foot at the target. Perfect hit! Then the right foot found its target, too! Another perfect hit! The left rear foot kicked out and ....another perfect hit! Kitty Wappis turned his body in mid air the required ¼ turn and...he was falling fast now...and kicked out at the one remaining target. The target wobbled to one side but didn't fall down! The audience gasped! The target wobbled in the other direction....and fell! The audience applauded loudly! But.......Kitty Wappis was not finished! He had to land perfectly on all four feet and be in the proper stance for the next move! HE DID IT! The audience applauded even louder this time! Kitty Wappis bowed to the judges and left the stage.

Kitty Wappis was very proud of himself. Kitty Wappis was very thankful and proud of his two very best friends, too! Kitty Wappis had walked off the stage smiling ear to ear! (Have you ever seen a kitty cat smile?)

The end of another purr-fect adventure.

Episode 17: THE CAT BURGLAR

Kitty Wappis had already finished his early morning Feline Karate practicing. Although he had earned the coveted Black Scarf, 3rd degree – the very highest level possible in Feline Karate – he always liked to stay mentally and physically fit. You, too? Kitty Wappis had watched the full moon set and, later, watched the sun rise while he read the morning newspaper. He often waited for the sun to warm his cushion – in his special bridge with lots of windows – so he could take his mid- morning catnap.

Kitty Wappis climbed to his cushion – in his special bridge with lots of windows. He stretched out his little toe to test the temperature of his cushion. HMMmm, JUST PERFECT! Kitty Wappis tiptoed onto his cushion, turned around twice, and plopped down right smack in the middle of that sunbeam! He curled into a ball, tucked his nose under his tail, closed his eyes, and went instantly asleep! Can you fall asleep that fast?

Kitty Wappis was barely awake from his refreshing mid-morning catnap. One eye was open and the other eye…well, he was still thinking about that! As he looked slowly out of the window he caught a glimpse of something moving. Something was moving in an area where something shouldn't be moving! Kitty Wappis fully opened his other eye. He studied the area very closer.

THERE IT WAS AGAIN!

LO and BEHOLD! HOLY COW! (and cats, too!) and TWO BIG MEOWS!

IT WAS A BLACK CAT! The sneaky cat below was moving in and out of the shadows. He (or she) was building something. Kitty Wappis watched from behind his curtain. The black cat was building something very unusual! It wasn't a ladder, but it was something to hoist that black cat either to the roof – or even to the special bridge with lots of windows! The contraption now had a long arm and some heavy framework. Kitty Wappis had excellent eyesight but this was very hard for him to believe! It was a cat-a-pult! It was being constructed to swing that black cat to the roof! This was a…a…..a…CAT BURGLAR! And…and…and, in the middle of the day, too! HOW DARING! This cat burglar had to be a very strange kitty cat! Well, Kitty Wappis was a very strange kitty cat, too!

Kitty Wappis could walk upright on his hind feet with his tail swishing back and forth and from side to side. Sometimes, when he walked upright, his upper torso would lean. Sometimes, he would LEAN to the right. Sometimes, he would LEAN to the left. Sometimes, when his tail was on the same side he was leaning, one would think that he would just fall over….but, he never did!

Kitty Wappis had a bird's eye view of this cat burglar. One might even say that Kitty Wappis was in the CATBIRD'S seat!

Could that CAT-A-PULT propel that cat burglar to the roof? Along the roof edge of the house belonging to Mr. Alexander P. Frockmorton III was a small catwalk. That cat burglar could gain access to the house from there. Kitty Wappis was a very smart kitty cat. Kitty Wappis studied the angle of that cat-a-pult and drew an invisible line. That cat-a-pult was aimed to propel that cat burglar to the house next door. That house was owned by Mr. J. Cobb (G.O.E.). It was rumored that there were hidden treasures in some cat-a-combs under both houses, but the entrances were never found.

Kitty Wappis left his special bridge. He was very quiet and quick. He snuck to the den belonging to Mr. J. Cobb (G.O.E.). Kitty Wappis watched that cat burglar. That long arm of the cat-a-pult propelled that black cat to the windowsill outside the den. Kitty Wappis strained his eyes and ears and studied that cat burglar. He (or she) was carrying a large bag. Then, he (or she) slid open the window. That cat burglar began collecting some valuable gold candlesticks and other items. He (or she) placed them carefully into that large bag. The cat burglar didn't see Kitty Wappis!

Kitty Wappis heard some footsteps in the outer hallway. Mr. J. Cobb (G.O.E.) was home and just outside the den door.

KITTY WAPPIS MADE HIS MOVE!

Kitty Wappis sprang from the shadows just as Mr. J. Cobb (G.O.E.) opened the door. The cat burglar dropped his (or hers) large bag as Kitty Wappis stood only inches from him (or her). Kitty Wappis was in the FELINE KARATE SELF-DEFENSE PALM STRIKE POSITION and fully upright on his hind feet! Kitty Wappis looked very frightening!

The cat burglar was so surprised that he (or she) appeared stunned. One might say that the cat burglar was in a cat-a-tonic trance! He (or she) didn't move a whisker!

Mr. J. Cobb (G.O.E.) secured that daring, daytime cat burglar and called the police!

Kitty Wappis was very proud of the fact that he had stopped that cat burglar! Kitty Wappis was so happy that he caught that cat burglar that he smiled all the way back to his cushion! Have you ever seen a kitty cat smile?

The end of another purr-fect adventure.

Episode 18: MINIATURE GOLF

Kitty Wappis was very comfortable on his warm cushion – in his special bridge with lots of windows. The sun was very warm and Kitty Wappis had just turned around to warm his back. He wanted to be just like you; cozy and warm in bed! How wonderful that felt! For Kitty Wappis, it was his mid-morning catnap!

Today was to be a very special day. Mr. Alexander P. Frockmorton III was having a birthday party for Mr. J. Cobb (G.O.E.). Mr. Alexander P. Frockmorton III had invited Mr. O. and his twin cats, Sherlock and Spurlock, and Samantha, and Jake, and Koko, and, of course, Kitty Wappis! There were to be two special guests, too, Kim and her son Jacob (age 6). This afternoon everyone was going to the miniature golf course! Mr. Alexander P. Frockmorton III had rented it for the whole day! It would really be fun! Have you ever played miniature golf? Have you ever seen any kitty cats play miniature golf?

It was such a beautiful day that Kitty Wappis and Mr. J. Cobb (G.O.E.) decided to walk. It wasn't very far – just across the city park and they could meet Mr. O. and his twin cats, Sherlock and Spurlock there, too. Mr. Alexander P. Frockmorton III was driving to meet his friend Kim and her son Jacob (age 6). Also, he had to get the special birthday gift!

Everyone met at the front entrance of the miniature golf course at noon. Mr. Alexander P. Frockmorton III carried a long, skinny, brightly wrapped package. It was the birthday present! Everyone wanted Mr. J. Cobb (G.O.E.) to open his present before the golf game began. Mr. J. Cobb (G.O.E.) carefully unwrapped the present. It was a Boberg 3 and ¼ golf club putter. It was just the perfect present! He thanked everyone and said he couldn't wait to try it today!

They all drew numbers from a hat to make pairs and decide the order of play. Kitty Wappis was paired with Mr. J. Cobb (G.O.E.) and they were the last pair to play.

Kitty Wappis had never played this game before so he watched every detail very carefully.

The golf course began with hole #1 and ended with hole #9. There was another hole, too. It was just for the winner of the game. It was called THE WATERING HOLE because water would spout out from the top of the tower. Some of the holes had different obstacles blocking the hole to make it harder to get that little ball in the hole. Some holes looked very easy and some looked very hard. The player with the least amount of swings, or strokes, to get the ball in each hole would be the winner. The winner is the only one that could try to get the ball in THE WATERING TOWER to win an additional prize!

Kitty Wappis was a very strange kitty cat. Kitty Wappis could walk upright on his hind feet with his tail swishing back and forth and from side to side. Sometimes, when he walked upright, his upper torso would lean. Sometimes, he would LEAN to the right. Sometimes, he would LEAN to the left. Sometimes, when his tail was on the same side he was leaning, one would think that he would just fall over….. but, he never did!

Soon everyone was playing. Kitty Wappis was having a terrible time. He would hit the ball and it would go in every direction except the right one! Sometimes the ball would bounce off the sides, or just stop and spin. Mr. J. Cobb (G.O.E.) was using his brand new Boberg 3and ¼ golf club putter. He was an excellent miniature golf player. His score was the best!

Everyone was very excited that Mr. J. Cobb (G.O.E.) won the game… especially on his birthday! He could now try to win another prize at THE WATERING HOLE!

THE WATERING HOLE looked very scary. It was over 8 feet tall. It had a rotating red light at the top that would flash when somebody got the ball into the hole. There was a siren, too. The tower had a window in the front with little metal shelves behind it. If the ball entered the tower it would climb those little metal shelves to the very top.

Mr. J. Cobb (G.O.E.) placed the special ball on the platform, or Tee. The platform rotated and moved up and down. Mr. J. Cobb (G.O.E.) needed perfect timing to hit the ball with his brand new Boberg 3 and ¼ golf club putter. He took the proper stance over the ball and studied the platform. He took careful aim and swung his brand new Boberg 3 and ¼ golf club putter. He hit the ball perfectly! The crowd yelled and applauded! That special ball went directly down the middle of the course.....then it stopped! Then, it went sideways! Then, it went backwards! The crowd was stunned! That special ball rolled to a little water pond, spun around twice, and stopped completely! THE WATERING HOLE tower lit up with every light bulb it had! Then a booming voice said "STROKE #1. PLEASE TRY AGAIN". The crowd gasped and sighed. There were only two strokes left!

Mr. J. Cobb (G.O.E.) aligned himself over that special ball once again. He swung his brand new Boberg 3 and ¼ golf club putter. That special ball moved itself completely out of the way of that putter! THE WATERING HOLE tower lit up once again. "STROKE #2. PLEASE TRY AGAIN".

Mr. J. Cobb (G.O.E.) took very careful aim this time and swung his brand new Boberg 3 and ¼ golf club putter. He hit that special ball so hard it flew directly into the hole near the bottom of THE WATERING HOLE tower. The crowd yelled and cheered! THE WATERING HOLE tower was silent! What happened? Kitty Wappis saw it first. That special ball was climbing those little metal shelves inside the window. The crowd gasped! That special ball was now at the top of the tower!

The siren BLARED! The lights FLASHED! The top of the tower EXPLODED with fireworks and WATER! Mr. J. Cobb (G.O.E.) had HIT the jackpot! The crowd ROARED! The jackpot prize was a gift certificate for lunch at a nearby restaurant for everyone!

Kitty Wappis was so proud of Mr. J. Cobb (G.O.E.) that he smiled all the way to the restaurant. Have you ever seen a kitty cat smile?

The end of another purr-fect adventure.

Episode 19: THE DISCOVERY….Part 1 of 2

Kitty Wappis was very comfortable in the morning sun. It had warmed his cushion in his special bridge with lots of windows. Kitty Wappis had just awakened from his mid-morning catnap. He often watched the full moon set, then did a crossword puzzle or two before eating his breakfast. He would sometimes practice playing his three-ba! musical instrument or practice his Feline Karate moves. Although he had earned the coveted Black Scarf, 3rd degree – the highest possible level – had always liked to stay in tiptop mental and physical condition. You, too?

Kitty Wappis had another adventure beginning soon and he needed to be in top physical condition. Kitty Wappis was going underground cave exploring. It was called SPELUNKING! It could be very dangerous so extra precautions were to be practiced as much as possible. The group Kitty Wappis was in were doing their first underground expedition this afternoon.

The safety exercise class went very well. Kitty Wappis learned many things about caves, too. Most importantly, he learned about how to use and maintain the proper equipment. Also, SPELUNKING is something that one must never do alone. It is always a team effort. Kitty Wappis had a nice lesson today but he was ready for dinner and a nice long sleep!

Kitty Wappis told Mr. J. Cobb (G.O.E.) and Mr. Alexander P. Frockmorton III (his two very best friends that he lives with) about his experience with SPELUNKING. They were truly amazed! Kitty Wappis was always trying something! His two best friends told him about the old rumors regarding underground caves and the tunnels and cat-a-combs nearby. These cat-a-combs were supposed to contain hidden treasures from centuries past! Nobody had ever been able to find any access to these caves, or cat-a-combs. Mr. J. Cobb (G.O.E.) often laughed about these rumors because the entrances were supposedly located right in his kitchen! Kitty Wappis was very amazed, excited, and curious! (Aren't all kitty cats curious?)

The next morning Kitty Wappis was climbing to his cushion for his mid-morning catnap. He stretched out his little toe to test the temperature of his cushion. HMMmm, JUST PERFECT! Kitty Wappis tiptoed onto his cushion, turned around twice, and plopped down right smack in the middle of the sunbeam! He curled into a ball, tucked his nose under his tail, closed his eyes, and went ALMOST to sleep…when the phone rang!

The answering machine clicked on and recorded the message..VERY LOUDLY! Kitty Wappis could hear the voice all the way up to his cushion. It sounded very familiar! Kitty Wappis tried to ignore it but that LOUD BOOMING VOICE was….could it really be?

Kitty Wappis perked both ears up! Then he stood up!

IT WAS HIS COUSIN! It was The Right Reverend Catty Van Meter from Kentucky ! And…he is on his way over to the house to see Kitty Wappis right now!

The Right Reverend Catty Van Meter was a Southern Feline Minister. He was primarily a Circuit Preacher. That meant that he had many small congregations – but many, many of them, and had to travel to each one. Catty – as Kitty Wappis remembered him – was quite a character! He always carried a small walking cane and wore a white suit and a hat. Catty always was a natty dresser! Catty carried a little Bible inside his left coat pocket. Once you ever met The Right Reverend Catty Van Meter, THE PREACHER, you would never forget the experience! Catty was a real character, no doubt about it!

Kitty Wappis and his cousin talked for many hours. Catty talked about his

"Feline Flocks" – as he liked to call his different congregations! When Catty heard about Kitty Wappis and his achievements....and the achievements of his sisters – Catty talked some more! Kitty Wappis could hardly squeeze a word in sideways! Finally, Kitty Wappis talked about his new interest in SPELUNKING and the rumored hidden cat-a-combs under this very house. Catty sat up and took notice! Catty took a long hard look at Kitty Wappis! Kitty Wappis took a long hard look at his cousin! Almost instantly they decided to search for the rumored hidden treasures! It was agreed that after all the expenses, the treasures, if any, would be given to charities.

They plotted their moves carefully. They would begin in the morning! They certainly were excited and curious! (Aren't all kitty cats curious?)

Kitty Wappis, The Right Reverend Catty Van Meter, Mr. J. Cobb (G.O.E.), and Mr. Alexander P. Frockmorton III poured over mountains of data, and documents, and maps, and satellite images, old blueprints, old newspaper articles and pictures, drawings, and anything else they could to find any clues and help them in their search for the hidden treasures.

Kitty Wappis and Mr. J. Cobb (G.O.E.) began their search in the den. Mr. Alexander P. Frockmorton III and Catty began their search in the cellar. They tapped on walls. They scraped off paint. They moved heavy furniture. They moved many boxes! They used sensitive electronic sensing devices! They tried everything! They found no clues; Nothing!...Nada!...Zilch!...Zero!...How frustrating!

Catty Van Meter plopped his exhausted body onto a blanket and located his Bible. Kitty Wappis plopped down and wiped his brow! Mr. J. Cobb (G.O.E.) and Mr. Alexander P. Frockmorton III sat down to drink some tea. It was time to re-plan and regroup!

Suddenly, Catty jumped up! He thought he was bitten by a mouse! He saw that mouse, mumbled some words from the Bible, and chased that mouse all over the room! The mouse disappeared like magic in the middle of the floor! Kitty Wappis found a small hole in the floor under some carpet. Mr. Alexander P. Frockmorton III fetched a powerful light but the hole was too small and too deep. Kitty Wappis tied a small weight on some twine and lowered it in the hole. It went down….and down…..and down. It finally clunked to a stop! The string measured over 30 feet long! WOW! WHAT AN AMAZING DISCOVERY!!

After some discussion and planning, it was decided to cut a hole in the floor large enough for Kitty Wappis and some of his new SPELUNKING equipment. Mr. J. Cobb (G.O.E.) fashioned a tripod with a pulley and a rope to raise and lower Kitty Wappis.

Kitty Wappis was connected to a harness and the rope and wore his special SPELUNKING safety equipment. He checked his two-way radio and his lights and began his journey! Kitty Wappis was lowered TEN FEET, then another TEN FEET, then another TEN FEET, then CLUNK!

Kitty Wappis was standing on a brick floor! With his excellent eyesight, Kitty Wappis saw the brick floor everywhere. He studied the floor but something was strange about this floor. It seemed to slope away from him on both sides! Kitty Wappis remembered his SPELUNKING training and counted his steps. First, he checked his compass for the proper bearings then went left twenty paces. He detected a severe slope in the floor. Then, he returned to his starting point and went twenty paces in the opposite direction. He detected a severe slope in the floor there, too. Kitty Wappis thought he might be on top of a tunnel. The brick floor could actually be the top of the ceiling of a tunnel below him.

Kitty Wappis checked his light and compass. Kitty Wappis checked his radio connection to his friends. Kitty Wappis moved 30 paces to the north. Then, 50 more paces. Then he returned to his starting point and went 100 paces to the south. Kitty Wappis noticed the temperature rising the farther south he went. He was going up hill! Kitty Wappis checked his maps and chatted with Mr. J. Cobb (G.O.E.) on the radio. Kitty Wappis returned to the room. Kitty Wappis now believed he knew where the long-lost entrances to the cat-a-combs were located! Kitty Wappis was a very smart kitty cat!

Kitty Wappis was a very strange kitty cat. Kitty Wappis could walk upright on his hind feet with his tail swishing back and forth and from side to side. Sometimes, when he walked upright, his upper torso would lean. Sometimes, he would LEAN to the right. Sometimes, he would LEAN to the left. Sometimes, when his tail was on the same side he was leaning, one would think that he would just fall over… but, he never did!

Although Kitty Wappis was a very smart kitty cat, more research would be necessary to continue this adventure…but, at least he was smiling. Have you ever seen a kitty cat smile?

Not quite the end of another purr-fect adventure…….

Episode 20: THE SOLUTION....Part 2 of 2

Kitty Wappis thought and thought about the ceiling of the tunnels he had walked on 30 feet below the floor of the den. What were they? How did they get there? What had they been used for? Where were the entrances and the exits to these mysterious tunnels?

Kitty Wappis, Mr. J. Cobb (G.O.E.), Mr. Alexander P. Frockmorton III, and The Right Reverend Catty Van Meter poured over all the information they had collected about the cat-a-combs (or tunnels). They spent many hours and days formulating plans and ideas.

Kitty Wappis had walked the entire length of that brick ceiling. It was over one mile long! It began around the old waterfront district. It ended exactly 172 paces from the hole where Kitty Wappis first entered by the rope with his SPELUNKING equipment. Kitty Wappis checked, re-checked, and double checked all of his notes and measurements. He, simply put, must have missed SOMETHING! Kitty Wappis must return to the cat-a-combs and try again!

Kitty Wappis collected his SPELUNKING equipment. Mr. J. Cobb (G.O.E.) connected the rope to the harness and lowered Kitty Wappis through the hole in the floor. TEN FEET! TWENTY FEET! THIRTY FEET and STOP! Kitty Wappis was standing on the bricks once again!

Kitty Wappis counted out the paces directly north and soon arrived at the end of the brick tunnel against a solid wall. EXACTLY 172 paces! There were some large concrete pillars along the edge of the tunnel. Kitty Wappis used his small hammer and tapped on the side of the first pillar. It sounded and felt very solid! He tapped on the side of the second pillar. It sounded and felt very solid, too! He tapped on the side of the third pillar and..................

LO and BEHOLD! HOLY COW! (and cats, too!) and TWO BIG MEOWS!

Kitty Wappis almost fell inside the pillar!

Kitty Wappis used his powerful lights to look inside the pillar. The pillar was almost entirely hollow! Kitty Wappis made his access hole wider and looked again. He found a spiral staircase! The spiral staircase went up and up and up and finally stopped at a flat ceiling! Kitty Wappis climbed the spiral staircase to the very top and found a very heavy door in the ceiling! It was much too heavy and stuck for him to move! Kitty Wappis made many measurements then returned the same way he had come. This was an exciting discovery, indeed!

Kitty Wappis was a very smart kitty cat. Kitty Wappis had studied all the collected information. He then thought that the ends of the tunnels (or cat-a-combs) had been sealed off because of the subway routes and utility lines. He also thought that the other end of the tunnels went to the old warehouse districts near the waterfront. Those old warehouses had been renovated into businesses and homes many, many years ago.

Kitty Wappis stood outside on the sidewalk. He was looking directly at an old stone church. Kitty Wappis had counted the paces and they led him to this church. He must enter and search that church for that heavy door. Can you imagine a very strange kitty cat, walking upright, going into a church carrying a tape measure, a notebook, and a compass?

Kitty Wappis was a very strange kitty cat! Kitty Wappis could walk upright with his tail swishing back and forth and from side to side. Sometimes, when he walked upright, his upper torso would lean. Sometimes, he would LEAN to the right. Sometimes, he would LEAN to the left. Sometimes, when he tail was on the same side he was leaning, one would think that he would just fall over…but, he never did!

Kitty Wappis was counting all the paces. He counted out the full 172 paces out loud and stopped at the very back of the altar. He looked and looked. No door anywhere! He double checked all of his notes and measurements. He double checked the compass reading, too! Kitty Wappis opened an old cloakroom door….. and….THERE IT WAS! It was almost invisible in the shadows! Kitty Wappis found the rusted hinges and the hasp! It was THE door in the floor!

Behind the church was a small rectory, or house. Beyond this house was a cemetery mostly hidden by large thick hedges. Beyond the cemetery were some old railroad tracks. Kitty Wappis saw all this from a small window inside the church. Kitty Wappis NOW knew about the cat-a-combs, or tunnels. Kitty Wappis NOW knew about the hidden spiral staircase inside the pillar, and about the door in the floor, and about the Rectory, and about the nearly hidden cemetery, and about the railroad tracks. He had also discovered the 9 square panels in the ceiling of the church. NOW it all made perfect sense!

This was a route for the Underground Railroad of years ago! The Underground Railroad was the secret passageway, or "safe" routes, for people escaping from the Southern states! They were seeking various freedoms and had to flee, then hide during the daytime. They would travel only at night using these "safe" routes where they could find food and shelter. The 9 panels in the ceiling of the church were called "quilts" and they could be hung outside to indicate the "safe" houses. Kitty Wappis was a very smart kitty cat!

To Kitty Wappis, Mr. Alexander P. Frockmorton III, Mr. J. Cobb(G.O.E.), and The Right Reverend Catty Van Meter, this was the true meaning of the hidden treasures of the mysterious, and lost, cat-a-combs under the house; FREEDOM!!!

Kitty Wappis was so happy he was smiling. Have you ever seen a kitty cat smile?

The end of another purr-fect adventure.

Episode 21: THE SKYDIVER

Kitty Wappis had just finished reading the morning newspaper. The sun was shining beautifully this morning and soon it would warm his cushion – in his special bridge with lots of windows. Kitty Wappis always looked forward to his mid-morning catnap. He had read an interesting story about skydiving this morning and he could dream about that very soon. This afternoon he was going to the park with Mr. Alexander P. Frockmorton III. Hopefully, Mr. O. would be there with his twin cats, Sherlock and Spurlock.

Kitty Wappis climbed to his cushion in his special bridge with lots of windows. He stretched out his little toe to test the temperature of his cushion. HMmmm, JUST PERFECT! Kitty Wappis tiptoed onto his cushion, turned around twice, and plopped down right smack in the middle of the sunbeam! He curled into a ball, tucked his nose under his tail, closed his eyes....decided to dream about skydiving....and went instantly asleep. Can you fall asleep that fast?

Kitty Wappis heard the noise of the airplane's engine. He looked around and saw at least five people. They were all wearing the same uniforms. They had helmets with visors and wind guards. Kitty Wappis saw his reflection in one of the helmet visors. He was wearing what appeared to be an orange and green "jump suit." He was also wearing some sort of high top leather shoes. He was wearing a helmet, too! Luckily, his visor was up so he could see! Kitty Wappis was strapped into some belted contraption – a harness with a large buckle on the front. There was an elongated ring that was hanging down next to that buckle. Kitty Wappis turned his head far enough to see that he was connected by all these belts and buckles to the front of someone.

Everyone stood up and put on gloves. Kitty Wappis had those high top leather shoes on all his feet so he didn't need any gloves! Someone reached over and lowered his visor. The world became very dark! It was time to jump out of the airplane! Kitty Wappis got closer and closer to that opened door! He could hear the air rushing past the door! Kitty Wappis watched as the first person jumped out of the airplane. Then another one jumped out. Then another! Now it was time for Kitty Wappis.......he was going sideways really fast! Then he started tumbling head over heels (kitty cats would probably tumble head over tails!) Kitty Wappis couldn't tell which end was up! All of a sudden he was going straight down toward the ground! Soon all of the skydiving jumpers joined hands in mid air! They looked like a giant snowflake! One skydiver released from the group and went straight up. Then another! Then another! Kitty Wappis saw their parachutes open. Then, FFOOOOOOFFFF!! Kitty Wappis went straight up too! The parachute unfolded and he felt as if he was floating in mid air....which, of course, he was!

LO and BEHOLD! HOLY COW! (and cats, too!) and TWO BIG MEOWS!

Kitty Wappis saw the ground coming up at him! He looked up and saw someone tugging on the ropes....Closer and closer.......PLOP! Kitty Wappis hit the ground. It was a little harder than necessary, he thought! (Remember, he IS dreaming.) Kitty Wappis had fallen off of his cushion onto the floor! Kitty Wappis awoke from his dream!

Kitty Wappis was a very strange kitty cat! Kitty Wappis lifted himself off the floor and met Mr. Alexander P. Frockmorton III for lunch and to go to the park.

Kitty Wappis was quite a sight to see! Kitty Wappis could walk upright on his hind feet with his tail swishing back and forth and from side to side. Sometimes, when he walked upright, his upper torso would lean. Sometimes, he would LEAN to the right. Sometimes, he would LEAN to the left. Sometimes, when his tail was on the same side he was leaning, one would think that he would just fall over...... but, he never did!

Kitty Wappis and Mr. Alexander P. Frockmorton III found Mr. O. and his twin cats, Sherlock and Spurlock. Today, Sherlock was talking about some exciting news. Mr. O. had rented a small airplane and they were going to try skydiving! What a coincidence! Kitty Wappis told them about the article in the newspaper he read this morning. He also told them about his dream. (He didn't tell them that he fell off of his cushion onto the floor!) Sherlock and Spurlock were amazed by the dream! Mr. O. and the twin cats were to begin the skydiving lessons tomorrow. Maybe Kitty Wappis would like to try to skydive instead of dreaming about it! Kitty Wappis couldn't wait to try it! (He still wasn't telling about falling off his cushion, but he was smiling!) Have you ever seen a kitty cat smile?

The end of another purr-fect adventure.

Episode 22: THE SERVICE DOG

It was another fine, sunny morning. Kitty Wappis had awakened very early this morning to see the full moon set. The bright, full moon was a very beautiful sight! Have you ever seen the full moon set in the western sky? Kitty Wappis remembered the time his friends had invited him to the Planetarium and Observatory. They had seen the full moon through the large telescope. They had seen many craters and hills. Afterwards, they even touched some of the moon rocks brought back by the astronauts! Kitty Wappis always enjoyed watching the full moon!

Now, Kitty Wappis was ready for his mid-morning catnap. He had eaten his breakfast and brushed his teeth. Then, he had waited for the rising sun to warm his cushion – in his special bridge with lots of windows. He had spent some extra time practicing his Feline Karate moves. Although he had earned the coveted Black Scarf, 3rd degree, he always wanted to be in tiptop mental and physical condition. You, too?

Kitty Wappis climbed to his cushion. He stretched out his little toe to test the temperature of his cushion. HMmmm, JUST RIGHT! Kitty Wappis tiptoed onto his cushion, turned around twice, and plopped down right smack in the middle of the sunbeam. He curled into a ball, tucked his nose under his tail, closed his eyes, and went instantly asleep. Can you fall asleep that fast?

Kitty Wappis was awakened by the sound of a barking dog. It seemed to be directly under his special bridge. Kitty Wappis opened both eyes and looked down to the street below. There was a big, black dog with a harness of some kind and a child in a wheelchair wearing a helmet. There was a yellow blanket draped over the dog's back, too. The reflective lettering on the yellow blanket had some words on it. They said "SERVICE DOG IN TRAINING". Kitty Wappis was fascinated, amazed, and curious (Aren't all kitty cats curious?). The dog seemed to know when to stop, when to go, and even looked in both directions before crossing the street! The dog barked each time it had done something different. Simply amazing! Kitty Wappis watched the dog and the child in the wheelchair until they were out of sight. The dog was a very strange sight to Kitty Wappis.

Kitty Wappis was a very strange sight, too. Kitty Wappis could walk upright on his hind feet with his tail swishing back and forth and from side to side. Sometimes, when he walked upright, his upper torso would lean. Sometimes, he would LEAN to the right. Sometimes, he would LEAN to the left. Sometimes, when his tail was on the same side he was leaning, one would think that he would just fall over…but, he never did!

Kitty Wappis and one of his best friends – Mr. J. Cobb (G.O.E.) - were supposed to go to the park this afternoon. [Mr. J. Cobb (G.O.E) always used those letters after his name. They meant "Gentleman of Ease". It meant that he wanted everyone to know he was retired from full time work!] Kitty Wappis hoped his friends, Mr. O. and his twin cats, Sherlock and Spurlock, would be at the park. The twin cats always had so much information! Kitty Wappis wanted to ask them about Service Dogs.

Kitty Wappis spotted Mr. O. (His bald head glistened in the sunlight!). The twin cats, Sherlock and Spurlock were nearby but slightly behind a tree.

As Mr. J. Cobb (G.O.E.) chatted with Mr. O., Kitty Wappis and the twin cats talked about the Service Dogs. As usual, the twin cats were just full of information! They told Kitty Wappis that the dogs were specially trained. They were usually big dogs because, sometimes, their extra strength was needed to help pull wheelchairs. Kitty Wappis listened very intently. The more information he heard, the more he thought that there must be a way for him to help in some way. He learned that the Service Dog training began when the dogs were little puppies. The special training necessary to become a Service Dog took as long as a whole year! The dogs were trained to do such things as open doors, answer the phone (They didn't really talk but could hold or deliver the phone!), turn on lights, and even get help in an emergency! Unfortunately, there were never enough trained dogs for all the people that really needed them! Mostly, the Service Dogs were trained by volunteers and their families. These wonderful volunteers helped with all the costs involved, too! Kitty Wappis listened and listened. There must be something he could do to help! These dogs seemed extra special and needed all the help they could get! (If you would like to help in any way, please contact your local county or State agency about Service Dogs for the Handicapped!)

Kitty Wappis was a very smart kitty cat. After returning from the park, he notified all of his friends. Kitty Wappis wanted to not only raise awareness of the existence of these much needed dogs, but also try to raise monies to help defray some of the expenses.

Kitty Wappis organized the Feline Marching Band members. Kitty Wappis talked with the city mayor. Kitty Wappis organized the local printers and the newspapers. Kitty Wappis even organized several Service Dogs to march in a parade! Kitty Wappis was quite an organizer, wasn't he?

Kitty Wappis was very proud of all his friends for trying to help the Service Dogs for the Handicapped.

Kitty Wappis was so proud of everyone that he smiled all the way back to his cushion for his mid-afternoon catnap! Have you ever seen a kitty cat smile?

The end of another purr-fect adventure.

The World Wide Web (the Internet) and your local agencies can provide a wealth of information regarding Service dogs for the handicapped and disabled. How can you help?"

Episode 23: THE TOOTHACHE

Kitty Wappis had just finished eating his breakfast. It was very early because he liked to watch the full moon set and practice his Feline Karate moves. (Although he had earned the coveted Black Scarf, 3rd degree – the very highest level possible – he liked to stay in tiptop mental and physical condition) Then he liked to play his three-ba! musical instrument. (Have you ever heard of the three-ba! musical instrument? It IS very rare!)

This morning he had already read the morning newspaper and did the crossword puzzle! Kitty Wappis was a very smart kitty cat! Sometimes, he did jigsaw puzzles, too. He could do those lickety split!

As he finished his breakfast he noticed a few little pangs of pain in one of his upper teeth. It wasn't too bad but it did ache a little more when he practiced his Feline Karate moves and maneuvers. Perhaps his mid-morning catnap would cure all the pangs and little aches! He usually ate his breakfast very slowly to give the morning sun a chance to warm his cushion – in his special bridge with lots of windows. It should be nicely warmed by now!

Kitty Wappis climbed to his cushion. He stretched out his little toe to test the temperature of his cushion. HMmm, JUST RIGHT! Kitty Wappis tiptoed onto his cushion, turned around twice, and plopped down right smack in the middle of the sunbeam! He curled into a ball, tucked his nose under his tail, closed his eyes, and was almost asleep when..........

LO and BEHOLD! HOLY COW! (and cats, too!) and TWO BIG MEOWS!

THE PAIN IN HIS TOOTH WOKE HIM UP!

Kitty Wappis must have been asleep a little while because when he tried to reach his face, his foot was asleep! Kitty Wappis flopped his foot over and twisted his ankle! Now he had two pains! He couldn't use his paw to hold his jaw! Not only was his jaw starting to throb, but his ankle, too! Kitty Wappis, very slowly, and quite painfully, crawled and limped his way to the kitchen. Mr. Alexander P. Frockmorton III was very surprised and dumbfounded by Kitty Wappis being in such pain. Mr. J. Cobb (G.O.E.) arrived for morning tea and was truly aghast when he saw Kitty Wappis! Mr. J. Cobb (G.O.E.) fetched a bag of frozen peas and molded the bag around the swollen ankle. Mr. Alexander P. Frockmorton III found an ice bag and tied it around the poor swollen face of Kitty Wappis!

Mr. Alexander P. Frockmorton III called Dr. Fred, his dentist. Mr. J. Cobb (G.O.E.) called Dr. Paul, the veterinarian and explained the emergency situation!

Kitty Wappis was taken to the dentist first. Dr. Fred examined Kitty Wappis and took several X-rays. Kitty Wappis had a severe infection under one tooth and a bad crack in another tooth! Dr. Fred treated Kitty Wappis the best he could and then referred him to Dr. Paul. Whatever Dr. Fred had done to Kitty Wappis, it sure worked! He was feeling much better already! He didn't need the ice pack anymore! (Sometimes, he rested his cheek on his paw though!)

Kitty Wappis hobbled into Dr. Paul's office with that frozen bag of peas wrapped around his ankle. He certainly was glad that Dr. Fred told him he didn't need the ice pack for his face! The ice pack was really not needed anyway. Dr. Fred told him that the blood flow to the tooth was slowed when he wore the ice pack. The tooth would get better faster without the ice pack. Has that ever happened to you?

Kitty Wappis was treated extra carefully by Dr. Paul. He had examined Kitty Wappis and taken some X-rays of his ankle. Luckily, no bones were broken. Time, ice, heat, and some physical therapy would heal the strained muscles and tendons.

THE TOOTH PROBLEM WAS A WHOLE DIFFERENT STORY! Dr. Paul would have to do some minor surgery to remove the cause of the infection in one tooth and prepare the other tooth for a hard covering called a crown.

Kitty Wappis had some pain relieving medication and a shot to numb his tooth. Only one tooth could be treated today. Kitty Wappis was soon on his way home with some medication to help fight the infection. Kitty Wappis would have to return in a few weeks to begin treatment on the other tooth. Mr. Alexander P. Frockmorton III and Mr. J. Cobb (G.O.E.) were very much relieved, too!

Kitty Wappis was a very strange kitty cat. Kitty Wappis could walk upright on his hind feet (when he didn't have a frozen bag of peas tied around his ankle) with his tail swishing back and forth and from side to side. Sometimes, when he walked upright his upper torso would lean. Sometimes, he would LEAN to the right. Sometimes, he would LEAN to the left. Sometimes, when his tail was on the same side he was leaning, one would think that he would just fall over....but, he never did!

Kitty Wappis felt much better and relieved as well! Kitty Wappis was very grateful and thankful to both Dr. Fred and Dr. Paul. Kitty Wappis promised himself to follow all their advice!

Kitty Wappis was very grateful for having two very best friends, too!

Kitty Wappis even managed a little smile as he drifted off to sleep. Have you ever seen a kitty cat smile?

The end of another purr-fect adventure.

Find the words listed below that are hidden in the puzzle.

The words may be upwards, downwards, sideways, or backwards!

CROWN	PAIN
DENTIST	SHOT
ICEPACK	SURGERY
INFECTION	TOOTH
JAW	X-RAY
KITTY WAPPIS	

Y	C	X	D	Y	R	E	G	R	U	S
K	Y	Z	E	T	J	A	W	F	M	H
P	A	I	N	B	Q	L	X	A	K	T
E	R	D	T	C	R	O	W	N	C	O
T	X	M	I	E	N	K	O	R	A	O
Z	V	O	S	H	O	T	P	A	P	T
C	H	V	T	B	D	F	N	J	E	I
I	N	F	E	C	T	I	O	N	C	X
S	I	P	P	A	W	Y	T	T	I	K

AAhhhsss...
Ooohhhss...

Episode 24: THE ITCH SCRATCHER

Kitty Wappis and Mr. J. Cobb (G.O.E.) went to the park very early this morning. Mr. J. Cobb (G.O.E.) enjoyed the early morning freshness of the grass and flowers. The aroma of the flowers was just wonderful! Don't you think so, too? Mr. J. Cobb (G.O.E.) often said that the early mornings in the park reminded him of being very young again. Maybe like you, perhaps?

Kitty Wappis liked to watch the birds fly from the pond. The park in the very early morning was very refreshing! Have you ever seen the early morning dew on the grass? Have you ever seen the early morning sunbeams streaming through a spider web?

Kitty Wappis always returned from the park just in time for his mid-morning catnap. Usually, Kitty Wappis watches the moon set in the west and the sun rise later from the east. Then he would eat his breakfast and practice his Karate moves. (He always wanted to stay in tiptop physical shape). Kitty Wappis had achieved the coveted Black Scarf, 3rd degree – the very highest achievement in Feline Karate! After his Feline Karate he would sometimes practice playing his three-ba! musical instrument? Have you ever heard of a three-ba! musical instrument? Have you ever heard of, or seen, a Two-ba! (Tuba)? Well, they are almost the same….but, then again, quite different! This morning going to the park with Mr. J. Cobb (G.O.E.) was an extra treat. Sometimes a special trip…even if it is just to the park, makes you feel much better! Right? You, too?

Kitty Wappis climbed to his cushion – in his special bridge with lots of windows. He stretched out his little toe to test the temperature of his cushion. HMmm, JUST RIGHT! Kitty Wappis tiptoed onto his cushion, turned around twice, and plopped down right smack in the middle of the sunbeam. He curled into a ball, tucked his nose under his tail, closed his eyes, and went instantly asleep. Can you fall asleep that fast? Kitty Wappis just started a very nice dream when……….

LO and BEHOLD! HOLY COW! (and cats, too!) and TWO BIG MEOWS!

Kitty Wappis had an itch on his back! As much as he tried, he couldn't reach that itch! Have you ever had an itch you couldn't reach? How frustrating! Kitty Wappis rolled over, twisted around, stretched his body in every possible direction, but still couldn't get at that elusive itch! Kitty Wappis was a very smart kitty cat. If he couldn't get at that itch, it was truly an elusive one!

Kitty Wappis was a very strange kitty cat. Kitty Wappis could walk upright on his hind feet with his tail swishing back and forth and from side to side. Sometimes, when he walked upright, his upper torso would lean. Sometimes, he would LEAN to the right. Sometimes, he would LEAN to the left. Sometimes, when his tail was on the same side he was leaning, one would think that he would just fall over… but, he never did!

Kitty Wappis walked upright to the doorway. He squished and squirmed his back against the edge of the door. He tipped, and leaned, and turned, and twisted his body so much, he looked like a pretzel! Kitty Wappis still could not reach that elusive itch!

Kitty Wappis sat on his tail and bent his legs behind him. He scratched with one foot as far as it could reach. Then he scratched with the other foot as far as it could reach! He moved his ears, tweaked his nose, stuck out his tongue, and twisted his whiskers but, still, nothing worked! Kitty Wappis just couldn't reach that elusive itch!

Kitty Wappis wriggled and danced to the kitchen. There, he found a long, wooden, salad fork. He held that salad fork in his front foot, slung it over his head toward his back and…..FOUND THAT ITCH!! Kitty Wappis scratched and scratched, and scratched again! Such relief! WOW! Are you sure you haven't had an itch like that? Ever?

Kitty Wappis decided that all kitty cats needed a special itch scratcher. It had to be very special. It had to reach from head to tail…and all spots in between! The next time he went to the park, he would be sure to find Mr. O. and his twin cats, Sherlock and Spurlock. He would ask them if they had ever had an itch that they couldn't reach.

Kitty Wappis decided to design and create the perfect itch scratcher just for kitty cats.

Kitty Wappis and his two best friends could work together on this project. Mr. Alexander P. Frockmorton III, Mr. J. Cobb (G.O.E.), and Kitty Wappis tried several different designs.

Kitty Wappis would turn, twist, tweak, and test each design. After all, he was the one that had that elusive itch that he couldn't reach! The group tried several more designs. Kitty Wappis squirmed, squealed, and squeaked! Nope, not yet! Kitty Wappis pulled, pushed, and punched. Nope…but much closer, he thought! They tried one last design for the day. It seemed perfect! Kitty Wappis oohed and aahed, and even purred! He tried it over and over. Each time it was perfect! It could reach wherever that elusive itch was hiding! It seemed to reach any itch, anywhere! It had a telescopic arm with three little claw fingers. The claw fingers could vibrate, and rub, or scratch, or even tickle! It was truly wonderful!

Kitty Wappis, Mr. Alexander P. Frockmorton III, and Mr. J. Cobb (G.O.E.) made several of these itch scratching devices. Kitty Wappis wanted to give one to Sherlock and one to Spurlock, too.

Kitty Wappis was a very strange kitty cat. Can you imagine a kitty cat that could walk upright on his hind feet? Or a kitty cat that could scratch an elusive itch with a brand new telescopic itch scratcher with three little vibrating claws? Or a kitty cat that turned, twisted, tweaked, and tested the designs for the itch scratcher? Or a kitty cat that pulled, pushed, pumped, and punched, to scratch an itch? Kitty Wappis was a very strange kitty cat, indeed!

Don't you think that Kitty Wappis was a very strange kitty cat? Can you imagine a kitty cat that could walk upright on his hind feet with his tail swishing back and forth and from side to side? AND, sometimes, when he walked upright, his upper torso would lean....especially if he couldn't reach that elusive itch! Sometimes, he would LEAN to the right - and use his new telescopic itch scratcher with the three little vibrating claws to scratch his itch! Sometimes, he would LEAN to the left - and scratch that itch, too! Sometimes, when his tail was on the same side he was leaning, one would think that he would just fall over....but, he never did!

Kitty Wappis could scratch that elusive itch now wherever it was! He didn't have to turn, or twist, or tweak! He didn't have to pull, or push, or pump, or punch, to scratch that elusive itch anymore!

Kitty Wappis even smiled each time he used his new telescopic itch scratcher with its three little vibrating claws.

Have you ever seen a kitty cat smile?

The end of another purr-fect adventure.

How do you scratch an itch when you can't reach it?

AAAAKERBERLISST-CHHOOOO!!!

Episode 25: THE TEA PROBLEM

Kitty Wappis had already finished his morning routine. He had watched the full moon set, watched the wonderful summer sun rise, practiced his Karate moves, eaten breakfast, brushed his teeth and still had a little time left to play his three-ba! musical instrument! Kitty Wappis had been busy all morning! Now it was time for his usual mid-morning catnap. He would often delay going to his special bridge with lots of windows because he wanted the morning sun to warm his cushion. It should be just right any minute now!

Kitty Wappis climbed to his cushion – in his special bridge with lots of windows – and checked his cushion. The sunbeam was exactly where it was supposed to be...directly in the middle! Kitty Wappis stretched out his little toe to test the temperature of his cushion. JUST RIGHT! Kitty Wappis tiptoed onto his cushion, turned around twice, then plopped down right smack in the very middle of the sunbeam. He curled into a ball, tucked his nose under his tail, closed his eyes and......and.........and...............and SNEEZED!

This was by no means just an ordinary sneeze. This was a BIGGIE!! This was the kind of sneeze that would wake entire neighborhoods! Kitty Wappis lifted his head way up – as far as it would go- wrinkled his nose, twisted his whiskers, braced himself with his front feet and.... and....KERBERLISTSSSSSTTTCCHHOO-OOO!!! That sneeze lifted his whole body right off the cushion! AAAAAAAA-KERBERLISTTSSST-CCHHOOOOOOOO!!!! He sneezed again and the window shades fell off the wall! Kitty Wappis sneezed so hard there were tears in his eyes!

HOLD ON TO YOUR HATS, HERE COMES ANOTHER ONE...... AAAAAA-

AAAAAA......AAAAAAA......KERBERSTSSSSSSSSST.... CHOOOOO!!! WOW!!! That one almost could blast your socks right off your feet!

Kitty Wappis picked himself off of the floor and found some tissues so he could blow his nose. Tears were running down his cheeks. His whiskers were twisted backwards and sticking to his face. His eyelids were drooping so much he almost couldn't see where he was going. Can you imagine? Have you ever sneezed like that?

Kitty Wappis was a very strange kitty cat. Kitty Wappis could walk upright on his hind feet with his tail swishing back and forth and from side to side. Sometimes, when he walked upright, his upper torso would lean – especially when he was sneezing! Sometimes, he would LEAN to the right. Sometimes, he would LEAN to the left .Sometimes - if he wasn't sneezing too hard – when his tail was on the same side he was leaning, one would think that he would just fall over....but, he never did!

Kitty Wappis made it as far as the big grandfather clock in the main hallway. His eyelids were almost closed. One ear was drooping backwards. His whiskers were sagging down. The other ear was bent forward. His nose was running everywhere. Kitty Wappis leaned his back against the wall, slid down to sit on his tail, lifted his head waaaayyy back, closed his eyes the rest of the way very tightly, took a deep breath and..........SNEEZED again!

Mr. Alexander P. Frockmorton III was in the kitchen just down the hall. He almost dropped his favorite tea cup! He was brewing some very special new tea. With his steaming cup of tea in one hand and a towel in the other hand, he peeked into the hallway. It was Kitty Wappis making all that noise! Mr. Alexander P. Frockmorton III looked at Kitty Wappis plopped against the wall. Kitty Wappis looked through his squinted eyes at Mr. Alexander P. Frockmorton III. Kitty Wappis saw the steaming tea cup and the towel. Kitty Wappis leaned his head back very quickly and sneezed again, and again, and once again. Kitty Wappis looked at the tea cup. Mr. Alexander P. Frockmorton III looked at the tea cup, too. Kitty Wappis struggled to his feet; took the tea cup and placed it outside near the door. Then, he covered his nose with the towel and went into the kitchen. They opened the windows and the back door. They turned on any fans they could find. They removed the rest of the tea from the house. Kitty Wappis was allergic to the tea!

Mr. Alexander P. Frockmorton III had just opened this tea this morning. It was Sassafras tea. It was supposed to have special healing properties......but, not for Kitty Wappis! WHEW!!

As soon as the tea aroma cleared, Kitty Wappis was beginning to feel better. His ears were finally bending in the right direction. His eyes were clearing. His nose stopped running. His tears stopped. His whiskers were almost normal again. He even began breathing better, too. Has that ever happened to you?

Mr. J. Cobb (G.O.E.) had heard all the commotion, too. When Kitty Wappis sneezed the very first time, Mr. J. Cobb (G.O.E.) looked outside to see if an airplane was flying too low! That sneezing sound had echoed throughout both houses! It had come from that special bridge – with lots of windows – down the stairs, through the den, and all the way to the basement where Mr. J Cobb (G.O.E.) was working. It had been very LOUD!

Mr. J. Cobb (G.O.E.) grabbed his steaming cup of tea and ran upstairs to check on Kitty Wappis as fast as he could. He had just brewed a new type of tea that was supposed to have many healing properties. Perhaps it would be exactly what Kitty Wappis needed. Perhaps this new green Sassafras tea...........................

The end of another purr-fect adventure.

Episode 26: FLOPPER BALL

The sun was shining very brightly this morning. Kitty Wappis couldn't wait for the sun to warm his cushion – in his special bridge with lots of windows. He was ready for his mid-morning catnap!

Kitty Wappis had watched the full moon set and the sun rise. They had both been spectacular! Kitty Wappis had eaten his breakfast, read the morning newspaper, did the crossword puzzle, put together some jigsaw puzzles lickety split, and even brushed his teeth.

Kitty Wappis climbed to his cushion. He stretched out his little toe to test the temperature of his cushion. HMmm, JUST RIGHT! Kitty Wappis tiptoed onto his cushion, turned around twice, and plopped down right smack in the middle of the sunbeam! He curled into a ball, tucked his nose under his tail, closed his eyes.... decided to dream about soccer....and went instantly asleep!

Kitty Wappis dreamed that he created a team of Feline soccer players. A real soccer team consisted of 11 players. Kitty Wappis would have only four or five kitty cats on each team. The soccer field, of course, would have to be much smaller, too. Kitty Wappis drifted into his deepest sleep and dreamed some more.......

Kitty Wappis was a very strange kitty cat. Kitty Wappis could walk upright on his hind feet with his tail swishing back and forth and from side to side. Sometimes, when he walked upright, his upper torso would lean. Sometimes, he would LEAN to the right. Sometimes, he would LEAN to the left. Sometimes, when his tail was on the same side he was leaning, one would think that he would just fall over.... but, he never did!

Kitty Wappis was dreaming that he was the goal tender and blocking many shots. He dreamed that he was the best goal tender because when he walked upright he could stop many shots!

Kitty Wappis dreamed about the size of the soccer field, too. He dreamed about the size of the soccer ball, too. After all, kitty cats were much smaller creatures! He also dreamed that his two very best friends could be the referees. Kitty Wappis was a very good dreamer, wasn't he?

Kitty Wappis dreamed about this new type of Feline soccer. It would be very similar to regular soccer but use a much smaller ball. This ball would have to be very special! Perhaps if it were shaped a bit different....hmmm. Maybe if it were flat on one side?? YES!!! Then, the new Feline soccer game could be called FLOPPER BALL! Then, FLOPPER BALL could be played on the FLOPPER FIELD! There would be two teams. Team A would be called THE FELINE FEDERATION FORUM FOURSOME. Team B would be called THE FELINE FRONTIER FORUM FOURSOME. Each team would have only four players and the goal tender. The goal tender would be called the FLICKER. The game would be played for 44 minutes and 4 seconds. (Remember, Kitty Wappis is still dreaming!) The team scoring the most goals would be the winner. The official timekeeper would be Mr. O. His twin cats, Sherlock and Spurlock, would be the team captains. One field official would be called the FIELD FOREMAN. This would be Mr. Alexander P. Frockmorton III. The other field official would be called the AFTMAN REFEREE. This would be Mr. J. Cobb (G.O.E.). The cheerleaders would be called THE FASHIONABLE, FLASHY, FELINE, FLOPPERETTES. (This is really quite a dream, isn't it?). Kitty Wappis was a very smart kitty cat!

Team A and Team B would meet in the center of the FLOPPER FIELD. The FLOPPER FIELD would only be forty yards long! The FLICKERS (goal tenders) would be in front on their nets. Each team must be in the proper FELINE-FORWARD-FOURSOME-FORMATION to begin the game. Samantha and Jake would toss in the FLAT-SIDED FLOPPER BALL to start the game. Kitty Wappis is one FLICKER and his friend, KoKo is the other FLICKER. The FLICKERS have to block that FLOPPER BALL from their goals.

THE GAME BEGAN!

The FELINE FEDERATION FORWARD FORUM FOURSOME (team A) was frequently formidable! The FLICKERS were awesome! They stopped the FLOPPER BALL many times! The FASHIONABLE, FLASHY, FELINE, FLOPPERETTES cheerleaders frazzled those FLOPPER BALL followers into a frenzy! The fans cheered and yelled and even whistled! (Have you ever heard a kitty cat whistle?)

THAT FLAT-SIDE FLOPPER BALL FLEW EVERYWHERE!

The FELINE FEDERATION FORUM FORWARD FOURSOME (Team A) flew that FLAT-SIDED FLOPPER BALL past KoKo (the FLICKER) and scored! The first score in fourteen minutes and forty-four seconds!

The teams rearranged themselves into the FELINE FORWARD FORMATION once again. Jake pitched that FLAT-SIDED FLOPPER BALL into the center of the FLOPPER FIELD and play began.

All of a sudden.....quick as a wink.........Team B (The FELINE FRONTIER FORUM) executed the perfect FLEA-FLICKER-FRIMSOL-FITCH-FLEET-FORCE maneuver and plopped that FLAT-SIDED FLOPPER BALL passed Kitty Wappis (the FLICKER) for a score! The FASHIONABLE, FLASHY, FELINE, FLOPPERETTES jumped around very loudly! The FLOPPER BALL followers cheered and yelled!

Samantha tossed that FLAT-SIDED FLOPPER BALL into the center of the FLOPPER FIELD. After only two flops and a plop, the official timekeeper blew his whistle. The FLOPPER BALL game was over! The game ended in a tie!

Can you even imagine a Feline soccer game? OR, a Feline soccer game ball that was flat on one side? OR, Feline cheerleaders called FASHIONABLE, FLASHY, FELINE, FLOPPERETTES? AND, what kind of special Feline soccer move is a FLEA-FLICKER-FRIMSOL-FITCH-FLEET-FORCE maneuver?

Kitty Wappis certainly was a good dreamer, wasn't he?

Kitty Wappis was very proud of everyone! Kitty Wappis was so proud that he awoke from his dream completely exhausted, but smiling from ear to ear!

Have you ever seen a kitty cat smile?

The end of another purr-fect adventure.

100
150
50
200
MPH
225 MPh
MIKE P.
KiTTY WAPPiS

Episode 27: THE RACE CAR

Kitty Wappis had finished breakfast and his Feline Karate practice. The full moon had set and he had seen the sun rise. Usually his cushion – in his special bridge with lots of windows – was warmed by the sun just about the time he was ready for his mid-morning catnap. Kitty Wappis felt the warm morning sun on his back as soon as he plopped down on his cushion. He had just closed his eyes................

VEROOM! VERVERVEROOM!!! VERRRRRROOOOOOMMMM!!??

What was that noise!!?? It felt like it was directly under Kitty Wappis. As the noise echoed through the streets, it actually shook the special bridge – with Kitty Wappis still in it! Kitty Wappis jumped off the cushion and peeked out the window. IT WAS A RACECAR!! It was zooming this way and that way! It was very fast and very loud!

All of a sudden that bright red racecar screeched to a stop. It was across the street from Kitty Wappis. The driver got out and removed his helmet. Kitty Wappis recognized the driver. It was none other than "Racer Mike P"! Mike P. was a very skilled Formula I and motorcycle race driver. Kitty Wappis hadn't seen Mike P. for such a long time.

What a pleasure to see an old friend again!

Mike P. was waving at Kitty Wappis to come down and see his new race car. Perhaps he could take Kitty Wappis for a little ride in it, too! Mr. J. Cobb (G.O.E.) and Mr. Alexander P. Frockmorton III came outside to see about all the noise. Mike P. was chatting with them when Kitty Wappis came down from his special bridge. Mike P. had an extra helmet for anyone that would like a demonstration ride. Mr. Alexander P. Frockmorton III and Mr. J. Cobb (G.O.E.) politely declined the offer.

Kitty Wappis climbed into the racecar, put on the helmet, and was snapped into what seemed to be 35 safety straps –it was really only 5!

Racer Mike P. started the powerful engine…..VEROOOM, VEROOOM, VEERRRROOOOOM!... AND AWAY THEY WENT!.... VERY, VERY, FAST! The buildings they passed were just a blur! Kitty Wappis couldn't feel his seat! Kitty Wappis was pushed so hard against the seat back he almost couldn't see out of his helmet. Mike P. told Kitty Wappis that he wouldn't drive too fast – until they arrived at the speedway. Kitty Wappis didn't know what to think; this speed was certainly plenty fast enough for him! When Mike P. asked him if everything was all right so far, Kitty Wappis couldn't even shake his head!

Racer Mike P. slammed on the powerful brakes of the racecar. The safety belts holding Kitty Wappis stretched to their limits! Kitty Wappis almost lost his helmet! The brakes screeched the racecar to a dead stop in mere seconds! Mike P. told Kitty Wappis that they were at the racetrack now and to hold on tight. Kitty Wappis didn't think he could hold on any tighter! Someone double checked all the safety equipment.

They even checked the helmet!

VEROOM! VERVEROOM!! VERVERVEROOOOOOMMM!!!

LO and BEHOLD! HOLY COW! (and cats, too!) and TWO BIG MEOWS!

That bright red racecar left the starting line in a cloud of smoke!

Kitty Wappis thought he was inside a rocket ship to the moon! Then, Racer Mike P. applied the brakes and slid sideways around the first turn. Kitty Wappis was told through the earphones in his helmet that was called a FOUR WHEEL DRIFT. Whatever it was called, Kitty Wappis was happy it was over! The racecar was now on the straight portion of the racetrack. It felt as if the car was tipping over onto its side. Racer Mike P. explained that because of the high speeds involved, the racetrack was BANKED, or raised up on one side. It helped keep the race cars on the track. The earphones in his helmet clicked on again. The announcer said that Racer Mike P. had driven the racecar over 240 miles per hour on the STRAIGHTAWAY! Kitty Wappis had just figured out what that meant when those brakes were slammed on again. Another turn! Another FOUR WHEEL DRIFT! And……Another STRAIGHTAWAY!!

Racer Mike P. slowed the mighty racecar to a crawl and finally stopped.

Kitty Wappis wasn't really sure that they were stopped. His head was still spinning and his back was aching. Soon he was out of the racecar and standing upright.

Kitty Wappis was a very strange kitty cat. Kitty Wappis could walk upright on his hind feet with his tail swishing back and forth and from side to side. Sometimes, when he walked upright his upper torso would lean. Sometimes, he would LEAN to the right. Sometimes, he would LEAN to the left. Sometimes, when his tail was on the same side he was leaning, one would think that he would just fall over……..but, he never did!

The other racecar drivers and the mechanics had never seen a kitty cat walk upright. They all thought it was because of the high speeds in the racecar that Kitty Wappis was still a bit dizzy!

Kitty Wappis just smiled to himself. Have you ever seen a kitty cat smile?

The end of another purr-fect adventure.

Episode 28: AN OLD GAME

The little white ball barely made it over the net. It was a real stretch for Kitty Wappis to get the paddle in place to return the little ball! He tapped it just out of the reach of KoKo.! Kitty Wappis scored the winning point!

KoKo served that little white ball again to start the second game. **PING! PONG!** And the ball was over the net to Kitty Wappis. He let the ball hit his side and drop off a bit to the side of the table. Kitty Wappis then used a little of his magic and sliced the ball at the same time he returned it to KoKo. The action of slicing the ball put some sort of side spin on that little white ball. When the ball hit the table on KoKo's side, it actually spun away from her. When she reached out to hit the ball, it wasn't there! It had bounced completely away from her! Kitty Wappis was an expert at doing this trick. (Mr. Alexander P. Frockmorton III showed Kitty Wappis how to this trick last night!) Another point for Kitty Wappis!

What Kitty Wappis didn't know was that KoKo had a trick or two of her own. She waited for Kitty Wappis to return a nice slow higher arcing ball. She knew that the ball was going to spin away from her. She calculated just how far she must reach out for the ball. KoKo brought her arm waaaayyyyy up and **SMASHED THAT BALL** back to the other side of the table! The ball was going so fast that Kitty Wappis didn't even see it! A point for KoKo! (Mr. J. Cobb (G.O.E.) showed KoKo how to do this trick last night!)

On the next serve to KoKo, she quickly moved to the side of the table and **SMASHED THAT BALL BACK** as soon as it hit her side of the table! Another point for KoKo! (Mr. O. showed KoKo how to do this trick last night, too!)

PING! PONG! SMASH! SSWWWOOOOSH! PING ! PONG! TICK, SMASH! PING ! PONG! SMASH! SWOOSH! PING ! PONG! SMASH! SWOOSH!......the game continued! PINGS AND PONGS WERE EVERYWHERE!

Kitty Wappis was beginning to get very tired! KoKo was just beating the daylights out of him! This was the last game and he was so far behind with points he was ready to give up! Where did she learn to play so well? She must have been just toying with him the first two games. Kitty Wappis had won the first game by a large margin. KoKo had managed to win the second game by the minimum of two points! This game was the hardest game of all! All the tricks that Kitty Wappis learned were not working! KoKo had the right answer for every trick that Kitty Wappis used! How did she do that?

Pingggg! Pongggg! SWOOOOOSH! Kitty Wappis swung at that little white ball and..........**missed!** The game was over! Koko was the winner!

KOKO WAS THE WINNER OF THE FIRST EVER FELINE TABLE TENNIS TOURNAMENT!

Everyone congratulated her! Everyone had a delightful time! The tournament had lasted the entire day!

Kitty Wappis had missed both of his catnap times! He was really tired now! He really struggled to climb to his cushion in his special bridge with lots of windows. The sun had set quite a long time ago so his cushion was not warm. Poor Kitty Wappis did NOT have to stretch out his little toe to test the temperature of his cushion. It was just as well anyway, because he was MUCH too tired! Poor Kitty Wappis did NOT have to tiptoe onto his cushion. Poor Kitty Wappis did NOT even have the energy to turn around twice......he just plopped down right smack in the middle of that cushion. Poor Kitty Wappis did NOT have enough energy to even curl into a ball or tuck his nose under his tail. He barely had enough energy to keep his eyes open..... GOODNIGHT KITTY WAPPIS!

BUT............KITTY WAPPIS COULD STILL DREAM!

Kitty Wappis dreamed about the Ping Pong tournament. Kitty Wappis dreamed about KoKo. Kitty Wappis dreamed that KoKo was teaching Kitty Wappis all the tricks on playing Ping Pong in a tournament. Kitty Wappis was so tired in this dream that he could not even hold the paddle correctly. Kitty Wappis was so tired that he found himself falling asleep when KoKo chased after the ball. Kitty Wappis was so tired that he put his head down right on the Ping Pong table! If there had been a cushion on the table top he might have climbed right up there!

Have you ever been that tired?

KoKo pretended to hit the ball to Kitty Wappis. Actually, she just bounced the ball under her paddle. She watched as Kitty Wappis slowly lifted his ping pong paddle. Kitty Wappis didn't have the slightest idea where the little white ball was! KoKo hit the ball under her paddle two more times. Kitty Wappis raised his ping pong paddle two more times. KoKo just couldn't hold back the laughter any longer! Kitty Wappis was a robot reacting to the sound of the ping pong ball! KoKo was laughing very hard! Kitty Wappis was still standing at the other end of the ping pong table with his eyes closed, mouth open, whiskers hanging, and the ping pong paddle raised in the air! Kitty Wappis was a sight to see!

Sometimes, he was actually smiling! Have you ever seen a kitty cat smile?

The end of another purr-fect adventure.

THE PURR-FECT END OF BOOK ONE

Answers to the scramble puzzle on page 41.

PICTURES	DOLLS
RADIO	TRUNK
BOOKS	SPIDERS
LAMP	TABLE

'ergne, TN USA
ıne 2010
909LV00004B/4/P